Reprint Publishing

FOR PEOPLE WHO GO FOR ORIGINALS.

www.reprintpublishing.com

[Page 17.

"CERTAINLY. I ASKED FOR ANOTHER CUP"

THE IDIOT

BY

JOHN KENDRICK BANGS

AUTHOR OF

"COFFEE AND REPARTEE" "THE WATER GHOST, AND OTHERS"
"THREE WEEKS IN POLITICS" ETC.

ILLUSTRATED

NEW YORK

HARPER & BROTHERS PUBLISHERS

1895

TO

WILLIAM K. OTIS

ILLUSTRATIONS

THE IDIOT

I

FOR some weeks after the happy event
which transformed the popular Mrs. Smithers
into the charming Mrs. John Pedagog all
went well at that lady's select home for single gentlemen. It was only proper that during the honey-moon, at least, of the happy
couple hostilities between the Idiot and his
fellow-boarders should cease. It was expect-
ing too much of mankind, however, to look
for a continued armistice, and the morning
arrived when Nature once more reasserted
herself, and trouble began. Just what it was
that prompted the remark no one knows, but
it happened that the Idiot did say that he
thought that, after all, life on a canal-boat
had its advantages. Mr. Pedagog, who had
come into the dining-room in a slightly irrita-
ble frame of mind, induced perhaps by Mrs.

Pedagog's insistence that as he was now part proprietor of the house he should be a little more prompt in making his contributions towards its maintenance, chose to take the remark as implying a reflection upon the way things were managed in the household.

"Humph!" he said. "I had hoped that your habit of airing your idiotic views had been put aside for once and for all."

"Very absurd hope, my dear sir," observed the Idiot. "Views that are not aired become musty. Why shouldn't I give them an atmospheric opportunity once in a while?"

"Because they are the sort of views to which suffocation is the most appropriate end," snapped the School-Master. "Any man who asserts, as you have asserted, that life on a canal-boat has its advantages, ought to go further, and prove his sincerity by living on one."

"I can't afford it," said the Idiot, meekly. "It isn't cheap by any manner of means. In the first place, you can't live happily on a canal-boat unless you can afford to keep horses. In fact, canal-boat life is a combination of the most expensive luxuries, since it combines yachting and driving with domesticity. Nevertheless, if you will put your

mind on it, you will find that with a canal-
boat for your home you can do a great many
things that you can't do with a house."

"I decline to put my mind on a canal-
boat," said Mr. Pedagog, sharply, passing his
coffee back to Mrs. Pedagog for another
lump of sugar, thereby contributing to that
good lady's discomfiture, since before their
marriage the mere fact that the coffee had
been poured by her fair hand had given it all
the sweetness it needed ; or at least that was
what the School-Master had said, and more
than once at that.

"You are under no obligation to do so,"
the Idiot returned. "Though if I had a mind
like yours I'd put it on a canal-boat and have
it towed away somewhere out of sight. These
other gentlemen, however, I think, will agree
with me when I say that the mere fact that a
canal-boat can be moved about the country,
and is in no sense a fixture anywhere, shows
that as a dwelling-place it is superior to a
house. Take this house, for instance. This
neighborhood used to be the best in town.
It is still far from being the worst neighborhood in town, but it is, as it has been for
several years, deteriorating. The establish-
ment of a Turkish bath on one corner and a

grocery-store on the other has taken away much of that air of refinement which characterized it when the block was devoted to residential purposes entirely. Now just suppose for a moment that this street were a canal, and that this house were a canal-boat. The canal could run down as much as it pleased, the neighborhood could deteriorate eternally, but it could not affect the value of this house as the home of refined people as long as it was possible to hitch up a team of horses to the front stoop and tow it into a better locality. I'd like to wager every man at this table that Mrs. Pedagog wouldn't take five minutes to make up her mind to tow this house up to a spot near Central Park, if it were a canal-boat and the streets were water instead of a mixture of water, sand, and Belgian blocks."

"No takers," said the Bibliomaniac.

"Tutt-tutt-tutt," ejaculated Mr. Pedagog.

"You seem to lose sight of another fact," said the Idiot, warming up to his subject. "If man had had the sense in the beginning to adopt the canal-boat system of life, and we were used to that sort of thing, it would not be so hard upon us in summer-time, when we have to live in hotels in order that we and our families may reap the benefits of a period

"THE NUISANCE OF HAVING TO PAY"

of country life. We could simply drive off to that section of the country where we desired to be. Hotels would not be needed if a man could take his house along with him into the fields, and one phase of life which has more bad than good in it would be entirely obliterated. There is nothing more disturbing to the serenity of a domestic man's mind than the artificial manner of living that prevails in most summer hotels. The nuisance of having to pay bills every Monday morning under the penalty of losing one's luggage would be obviated, and all the comforts of home would be directly within reach. The trouble incident upon getting the trunks packed and the children ready for a long day's journey by rail, and the fatigue arising from such a journey, would be reduced to a minimum. The troubles attendant upon going into a far country, and leaving one's house in the sole charge of a lot of servants for a month or two every year, would be done away with entirely; and if at any time it became necessary to discharge one of these servants, she could be put off the boat in an instant, and then the boat could be pushed out into the middle of the canal, so that the discharged domestic could not possibly get

aboard again and take her revenge by smash-
ing your crockery and fixtures. That is one
of the worst features of living in a stationary
house. You are entirely at the mercy of vin-
dictive servants. They know precisely where
you live, and you cannot escape them. They
can come back when there is no man around,
and raise several varieties of Ned with your
wife and children. With a movable house,
such as the canal-boat would be, you could
always go off and leave your family in perfect safety."

"How about safety in a storm?" asked the
Bibliomaniac.

"Safety in a storm?" echoed the Idiot.
"That seems an absurd sort of a question to
one who knows anything about canal-boats. I,
for one, never heard of a canal-boat being se-
riously damaged in a storm as long as it was
anchored in the canal proper. It certainly
isn't any more dangerous to be in a canal-
boat in a storm than it is to be in a house
that offers resistance to the winds, and is
shaken from roof to cellar at every blast.
More houses have been blown from their
foundations than canal-boats sunk, provided
ordinary care has been taken to protect
them."

"And you think the canal-boat would be healthy?" asked the Doctor. "How about dampness and all that?"

"That is a professional question," returned the Idiot, "which I think you could answer better than I. I don't see why a canal-boat shouldn't be healthy, however. The dampness would not amount to very much. It would be outside of one's dwelling, and not within it, as is the case with so many houses. A canal-boat having no cellar could not have a damp one, and if by some untoward circumstance it should spring a leak, the water could be pumped out at once and the leak plugged up. However this might be, I'll offer another wager to this board on that point, and that is that more people die in houses than on canal-boats."

"We'd rather give you our money right out," retorted the Doctor.

"Thank you," said the Idiot. "But I don't need money. I don't like money. Money is responsible for more extravagance than any other commodity in existence. Besides, it and I are not intimate enough to get along very well together, and when I have any I immediately do my level best to rid myself of it. But to return to our canal-boat. I note a look of disapproval in Mr. White-choker's eyes. He doesn't seem to think any more of my scheme than do the rest of you— which I regret, since I believe that he would be the gainer if land edifices were supplanted by the canal system as proposed by myself. Take church on a rainy morning, for in-stance. A great many people stay at home from church on rainy mornings just because they do not want to venture out in the wet. Suppose we all lived in canal-boats? Would not people be deprived of this flimsy pretext for staying at home if their homes could be towed up to the church door? Or, better yet, granting that the churches followed out the same plan, and were themselves constructed like canal-boats, how easy it would be for the sexton to drive the church around the town and collect the absentees. In the same man-ner it would be glorious for men like our-selves, who have to go to their daily toil. For a consideration, Mrs. Pedagog could have us driven to our various places of business every morning, returning for us in the evening. Think how fine it would be for me, for in-stance, instead of having to come home every night in an overcrowded elevated train or on a cable-car, to have the office-boy come and

"SHE COULD NOT POSSIBLY GET ABOARD AGAIN"

announce, 'Mrs. Pedagog's Select Home for Gentlemen is at the door, Mr. Idiot.' I could step right out of my office into my charming little bedroom up in the bow, and the time usually expended on the cars could be devoted to dressing for tea. Then we could stop in at the court-house for our legal friend; and as for Doctor Capsule, wouldn't he revel in driving this boarding-house about town on his daily rounds among his patients?"

"What would become of my office hours?" asked the Doctor. "If this house were whirling giddily all about the city from morning until night, I don't know what would become of my office patients."

"They might die a little sooner or live a little longer, that is all," said the Idiot. "If they weren't able to find the house at all, however, I think it would be better for us, for much as I admire you, Doctor, I think your office hours are a nuisance to the rest of us. I had to elbow my way out of the house this morning between a double line of sufferers from mumps and influenza, and other pleasingly afflicted patients of yours, and I didn't like it very much."

"I don't believe they liked it much either," returned the Doctor. "One man with a sprained ankle told me about you. You shoved him in passing."

"Well, you can apologize to him in my behalf," returned the Idiot; "but you might add that he must expect very much the same treatment whenever he and a boy with mumps stand between me and the door. Sprained ankles aren't contagious, and I preferred shoving him to the other alternative."

The Doctor was silent, and the Idiot rose to go. "Where will the house be this evening about six-thirty, Mrs. Pedagog?" he asked, as he pushed his chair back from the table.

"Where? Why, here, of course," returned the landlady.

"Why, yes—of course," observed the Idiot, with an impatient gesture. "How foolish of me! I've really been so wrapped up in my canal-boat ideal that I came to believe that it might possibly be real and not a dream, after all. I almost believed that perhaps I should find that the house had been towed somewhere up into Westchester County on my return, so that we might all escape the city's tax on personal property, which I am told is unusually high this year."

With which sally the Idiot kissed his hand to Mr. Pedagog and retired from the scene.

II

"Let's write a book," suggested the Idiot, as he took his place at the board and unfolded his napkin.

"What about?" asked the Doctor, with a smile at the idea of the Idiot's thinking of embarking on literary pursuits.

"About four hundred pages long," said the Idiot. "I feel inspired."

"You are inspired," said the School-Master. "In your way you are a genius. I really never heard of such a variegated Idiot as you are in all my experience, and that means a great deal, I can tell you, for in the course of my career as an instructor of youth I have encountered many idiots."

"Were they idiots before or after having drank at the fount of your learning?" asked the Idiot, placidly.

Mr. Pedagog glared, and the Idiot was apparently satisfied. To make Mr. Pedagog

glare appeared to be one of the chiefest of
his ambitions.

"You will kindly remember, Mr. Idiot,"
said Mrs. Pedagog at this point, "that Mr.
Pedagog is my husband, and such insinua-
tions at my table are distinctly out of place."

"I ask your pardon, Mrs. Pedagog," rejoined the offender, meekly. "Nevertheless,
as apart from the question in hand as to
whether Mr. Pedagog inspires idiocy or not,
I should like to get the views of this gather-
ing on the point you make regarding the
table. *Is* this your table? Is it not rather
the table of those who sit about it to regale
their inner man with the good things under
which I remember once or twice in my life to
have heard it groan? To my mind, the latter
is the truth. It is *our* table, because we buy
it, and I am forced to believe that some of us
pay for it. I am prepared to admit that if
Mr. Brief, for instance, is delinquent in his
weekly payments, his interest in the table re-
verts to you until he shall have liquidated,
and he is not privileged to say a word that you
do not approve of; but I, for instance, who
since January 1st have been compelled to pay
in advance, am at least sole lessee, and for
the time being proprietor of the portion for

which I have paid. You have sold it to me.
I have entered into possession, and while in
possession, as a matter of right and not on
sufferance, haven't I the privilege of freedom
of speech?"

"You certainly exercise the privilege
whether you have it or not," snapped Mr.
Pedagog.

"Well, I believe in exercise," said the
Idiot. "Exercise brings strength, and if ex-
ercising the privilege is going to strengthen
it, exercise it I shall, if I have to hire a gym-
nasium for the purpose. But to return to
Mrs. Pedagog's remark. It brings up another
question that has more or less interested me.
Because Mrs. Smithers married Mr. Pedagog,
do we lose all of our rights in Mr. Pedagog?
Before the happy event that reduced our
number from ten to nine—"

"We are still ten, are we not?" asked Mr.
Whitechoker, counting the guests.

"Not if Mr. Pedagog and the late Mrs.
Smithers have become one," said the Idiot.
"But, as I was saying, before the happy
event that reduced our number from ten to
nine we were permitted to address our friend
Pedagog in any terms we saw fit, and whenever he became sufficiently interested to in-

dulge in repartee we were privileged to return it. Have we relinquished that privilege? I don't remember to have done so."

"It's a question worthy of your giant intellect," said Mr. Pedagog, scornfully. "For myself, I do not at all object to anything you may choose to say to me or of me. Your assaults are to me as water is to a duck's back."

"I am sorry," said the Idiot. "I hate family disagreements, and here we have Mrs. Pedagog taking one side and Mr. Pedagog the other. But whatever decision may ultimately be reached, of one thing Mrs. Pedagog must be assured. I on principle side against Mr. Pedagog, and if it be the wish of my good landlady that I shall refrain from playing intellectual battledore and shuttlecock with her husband, whom we all revere, I certainly shall refrain. Hereafter if I indulge in anything that in any sense resembles repartee with our landlord, I wish it distinctly understood that an apology goes with it."

"That's all right, my boy," said the School-Master. "You mean well. You are a little new, that's all, and we all understand you."

"I don't understand him," growled the

Doctor, still smarting under the recollection of former breakfast-table discomfitures. "I wish we could get him translated."

"If you prescribed for me once or twice I think it likely I should be translated in short order," retorted the Idiot. "I wonder how I'd go translated into French?"

"You couldn't be expressed in French," put in the Lawyer. "It would take some barbarian tongue to do you justice."

"Very well," said the Idiot. "Proceed. Do me justice."

"I can't begin to," said Mr. Brief, angrily.

"That's what I thought," said the Idiot. "That's the reason why you always do me such great injustice. You lawyers always have to be doing something, even if it is only holding down a chair so that it won't blow out of your office window. If you haven't any justice to mete out, you take another tack and dispense injustice with lavish hand. However, I'll forgive you if you'll tell me one thing. What's libel, Mr. Brief?"

"None of your business," growled the Lawyer.

"A very good general definition," said the Idiot, approvingly. "If there's any business in the world that I should hate to have known as mine it is that of libel. I think, however, your definition is not definite. What I wanted to know was just how far I could go with remarks at this table and be safe from prosecution."

"Nobody would ever prosecute you, for two reasons," said the lawyer. "In a civil action for money damages a verdict against you for ten cents wouldn't be worth a rap, because the chances are you couldn't pay. In a criminal action your conviction would be a bad thing, because you would be likely to prove a corrupting influence in any jail in creation. Besides, you'd be safe before a jury, anyhow. You are just the sort of idiot that the intelligent jurors of to-day admire, and they'd acquit you of any crime. A man has a right to a trial at the hands of a jury of his peers. I don't think even in a jury-box twelve idiots equal to yourself could be found, so don't worry."

"Thanks. Have a cigarette?" said the Idiot, tossing one over to the Lawyer. "It's all I have. If I had a half-dollar I should pay you for your opinion ; but since I haven't, I offer you my all. The temperature of my coffee seems to have fallen, Mrs. Pedagog. Will you kindly let me have another cup?"

"Certainly, said Mrs. Pedagog. "Mary, get the Idiot another cup."

Mary did as she was told, placing the empty bit of china at Mrs. Pedagog's side.

"It is for the Idiot, Mary," said Mrs. Pedagog, coldly. "Take it to him."

"Empty, ma'am?" asked the maid.

"Certainly, Mary," said the Idiot, perceiving Mrs. Pedagog's point. "I asked for another cup, not for more coffee."

Mrs. Pedagog smiled quietly at her own joke. At hair-splitting she could give the Idiot points.

"I am surprised that Mary should have thought I wanted more coffee," continued the Idiot, in an aggrieved tone. "It shows that she too thinks me out of my mind."

"You are not out of your mind," said the Bibliomaniac. "It would be a good thing if you were. In replenishing your mental supply you might have the luck to get better quality."

"I probably should have the luck," said the Idiot. "I have had a great store of it in my life. From the very start I have had luck. When I think that I was born myself, and not you, I feel as if I had had more than my share of good-fortune—more luck than the law allows. How much luck does the law allow, Mr. Brief?"

"Bosh!" said Mr. Brief, with a scornful wave of his hand, as if he were ridding himself of a troublesome gnat. "Don't bother me with such mind-withering questions."

"All right," said the Idiot. "I'll ask you an easier one. Why does not the world recognize matrimony?"

Mr. Whitechoker started. Here, indeed, was a novel proposition.

"I—I—must confess," said he, "that of all the idiotic questions I—er—I have ever had the honor of hearing asked that takes the—"

"Cake?" suggested the Idiot.

"—palm!" said Mr. Whitechoker, severely.

"Well, perhaps so," said the Idiot. "But matrimony is the science, or the art, or whatever you call it, of making two people one, is it not?"

"It certainly is," said Mr. Whitechoker. "But what of it?"

"The world does not recognize the unity," said the Idiot. "Take our good proprietors, for instance. They were made one by yourself, Mr. Whitechoker. I had the pleasure of being an usher at the ceremony, yielding the

"DEMANDS TICKETS FOR TWO"

position of best man gracefully, as is my wont, to the Bibliomaniac. He was best man, but not the better man, by a simple process of reasoning. Now no one at this board disputes that Mr. and Mrs. Pedagog are one, but how about the world? Mr. Pedagog takes Mrs. Pedagog to a concert. Are they one there?"

"Why not?" asked Mr. Brief.

"That's what I want to know—why not? The world, as represented by the ticket-taker at the door, says they are not—or implies that they are not, by demanding tickets for two. They attempt to travel out to Niagara Falls. The railroad people charge them two fares; the hackman charges them two fares; the hotel bills are made out for two people. It is the same wherever they go in the world, and I regret to say that even in our own home there is a disposition to regard them as two. When I spoke of there being nine persons here instead of ten, Mr. White-choker himself disputed my point—and yet it was not so much his fault as the fault of Mr. and Mrs. Pedagog themselves. Mrs. Pedagog seems to cast doubt upon the unity by providing two separate chairs for the two halves that make up the charming entirety. Two cups are provided for their coffee. Two forks, two knives, two spoons, two portions of all the delicacies of the season which are lavished upon us out of season—generally after it—fall to their lot. They do not object to being called a happy *couple*, when they should be known as a happy single. Now what I want to know is why the world does not accept the shrinkage which has been pronounced valid by the church and is recognized by the individual ? Can any one here tell me that ?"

No one could, apparently. At least no one endeavored to. The Idiot looked inquiringly at all, and then, receiving no reply to his question, he rose from the table.

"I think," he said, as he started to leave the room—"I think we ought to write that book. If we made it up of the things you people don't know, it would be one of the greatest books of the century. At any rate, it would be great enough in bulk to fill the biggest library in America."

III

"I wish I were beginning life all over again," said the Idiot one spring morning, as he took his accustomed place at Mrs. Pedagog's table.

"I wish you were," said Mr. Pedagog from behind his newspaper. "Then your parents would have you shut up in a nursery, and it is even conceivable that you would be receiving those disciplinary attentions with a slipper that you seem to me so frequently to deserve, were you at this present moment in the nursery stage of your development."

"My!" ejaculated the Idiot. "What a wonder you are, Mr. Pedagog! It is a good thing you are not a justice in a criminal court."

"And what, may I venture to ask," said Mr. Pedagog, glancing at the Idiot over his spectacles—"what has given rise to that extraordinary remark, the connection of which with anything that has been said or done this morning is distinctly not apparent ?"

"I only meant that a man who was so given over to long sentences as you are would probably make too severe a judge in a criminal court," replied the Idiot, meekly. "Do you make use of the same phraseology in the class-room that you dazzle us with, I should like to know ?"

"And why not, pray ?" said Mr. Pedagog.

"No special reason," said the Idiot ; "only it does seem to me that an instructor of youth ought to be more careful in his choice of adverbs than you appear to be. Of course Doctor Bolus here is under no obligation to speak more grammatically or correctly than he does. People call him in to prescribe, not to indulge in rhetorical periods, and he can write his prescriptions in a sort of intuitive Latin and nobody be the wiser, but you, who are said to be sowing the seeds of knowledge in the brain of youth, should be more careful."

"Hear the grammarian talk !" returned Mr. Pedagog. "Listen to this embryonic Samuel Johnson the Second. What have I said that so offends the linguistic taste of Lindley Murray, Jun. ?"

"Nothing," returned the Idiot. "I can-

not say that you have said anything. I never
heard you say anything in my life ; but while
you can no doubt find good authority for
making use of the words 'distinctly not apparent,' you ought not to throw such phrases
around carelessly. The thing which is distinct is apparent, therefore to say 'distinctly
not apparent' to a mind that is not given to
analysis sounds strange. You might as well
say of a beautiful girl that she is plainly
pretty, meaning of course that she is evidently pretty ; but those who are unacquainted
with the idiomatic peculiarities of your speech
might ask you if you meant that she was
pretty in a plain sort of way. Suppose, too,
you were writing a novel, and, in a desire to
give your reader a fair idea of the personal
appearance of a homely but good creature,
you should say, 'It cannot be denied that
Rosamond Follansbee was pretty plain ?' It
wouldn't take a very grave error of the types
to change your entire meaning. To save a
line on a page, for instance, it might become
necessary to eliminate a single word ; and if
that word should chance to be the word
'plain' in the sentence I have given, your
homely but good person would be set down
as being undeniably pretty. Which shows,

it seems to me, that too great care cannot be exercised in the making of selections from our vocabu—"

"You are the worst I *ever* knew !" snapped Mr. Pedagog.

"Which only proves," observed the Idiot, "that you have not heeded the Scriptural injunction that you should know thyself. Are those buckwheat cakes or doilies ?"

Whether the question was heard or not is not known. It certainly was not answered, and silence reigned for a few minutes. Finally Mrs. Pedagog spoke, and in the manner of one who was somewhat embarrassed. "I am in an embarrassing position," said she.

"Good !" said the Idiot, *sotto-voce*, to the genial gentleman who occasionally imbibed. "There is hope for the landlady yet. If she can be embarrassed she is still human—a condition I was beginning to think she wotted not of."

"She whatted what ?" queried the genial gentleman, not quite catching the Idiot's words.

"Never mind," returned the Idiot. "Let's hear how she ever came to be embarrassed."

"I have had an application for my first-floor suite, and I don't know whether I ought to accept it or not," said the landlady.

"She has a conscience, too," whispered the Idiot ; and then he added, aloud, "And wherein lies the difficulty, Mrs. Pedagog?"

"The applicant is an actor ; Junius Brutus Davenport is his name."

"A tragedian or a comedian?" asked the Bibliomaniac.

"Or first walking gentleman, who knows every railroad tie in the country?" put in the Idiot.

"That I do not know," returned the land-lady. "His name sounds familiar enough, though. I thought perhaps some of you gentlemen might know of him."

"I have heard of Junius Brutus," observed the Doctor, chuckling slightly at his own humor, "and I've heard of Davenport, but Junius Brutus Davenport is a combination with which I am not familiar."

"Well, I can't see why it should make any difference whether the man is a tragedian, or a comedian, or a familiar figure to railroad men," said Mr. Whitechoker, firmly. "In any event, he would be an extremely objec—"

"It makes a great deal of difference," said the Idiot. "I've met tragedians, and I've met comedians, and I've met New York Central stars, and I can assure you they each represent a distinct type. The tragedians, as a rule, are quiet meek individuals, with soft low voices, in private life. They are more timid than otherwise, though essentially amiable. I knew a tragedian once who, after killing seventeen Indians, a road-agent, and a gross of cowboys between eight and ten P. M. every night for sixteen weeks, working six nights a week, was afraid of a mild little soft-shell crab that lay defenceless on a plate before him on the evening of the seventh night of the last week. Tragedians make agreeable companions, I can tell you ; and if J. Brutus Davenport is a tragedian, I think Mrs. Pedagog would do well to let him have the suite, provided, of course, that he pays for it in advance."

" I was about to observe, when our friend interrupted me," said Mr. Whitechoker, with dignity, " that in any event an actor at this board would be to me an extremely objec—"

" Now the comedians," resumed the Idiot, ignoring Mr. Whitechoker's remark—" the comedians are very different. They are twice as bloodthirsty as the murderers of the drama, and, worse than that, they are given to re-

"THEY ARE GIVEN TO REHEARSING AT ALL HOURS"

hearsing at all hours of the day and night.
A tragedian is a hard character only on the
stage, but the comedian is the comedian always. If we had one of those fellows in our
midst, it would not be very long before we
became part of the drama ourselves. Mrs.
Pedagog would find herself embarrassed once
an hour, instead of, as at present, once a century. Mr. Whitechoker would hear of himself as having appeared by proxy in a roaring
farce before our comedian had been with
us two months. The wise sayings of our
friend the School-Master would be spoken
nightly from the stage, to the immense de-
light of the gallery gods, and to the edifica-
tion of the orchestra circle, who would wonder how so much information could have got
into the world and they not know it before.
The out-of-town papers would literally teem
with witty extracts from our comedian's plays,
which we should immediately recognize as
the dicta of my poor self."

"All of which," put in Mr. Whitechoker,
"but proves the truth of my assertion that
such a person would be an extremely objec—"

"Then, as I said before," continued the
Idiot, "he is continually rehearsing, and his
objectionableness as a fellow-boarder would

be greater or less, according to his play. If he were impersonating a shiftless wanderer, who shows remarkable bravery at a hotel fire, we should have to be prepared at any time to hear the fire-engines rushing up to the front door, and to see our comedian scaling the fire-escape with Mrs. Pedagog and her account-books in his arms, simply in the line of rehearsal. If he were impersonating a detective after a criminal masquerading as a good citizen, the School-Master would be startled some night by a hoarse voice at his key-hole exclaiming : ' Ha ! ha ! I have him now. There is no escape save by the back window, and that's so covered o'er with dust 'twere suffocation sure to try it.' I hesitate to say what would happen if he were a tank comedian."

"Perhaps," said Mr. Whitechoker, with a trifle more impatience than was compatible with his calling—" perhaps you will hesitate long enough for me to state what I have been trying to state ever since this soliloquy of yours began—that in any event, whether this person be a tragedian, or a comedian, or a walking gentleman, or a riding gentleman in a circus, I object to his being admitted to this circle, and I deem it well to say right

"'HA! HA! I HAVE HIM NOW!'"

here that as he comes in at the front door I
go out at the back. As a clergyman, I do
not approve of the stage."

"That ought to settle it," said the Idiot.
"Mr. Whitechoker is too good a friend to
us all here for us to compel him to go out
of that back door into the rather limited
market-garden Mrs. Pedagog keeps in the
yard. My indirect plea for the admission
of Mr. Junius Brutus Davenport was based
entirely upon my desire to see this circle
completed or nearer completion than it is
at present. We have all the professions
represented here but the stage, and why ex-
clude it, granting that no one objects? The
men whose lives are given over to the amuse-
ment of mankind, and who are willing to
place themselves in the most outrageous situations night after night in order that we
may for the time being seem to be lifted out
of the unpleasant situations into which we
have got ourselves, are in my opinion doing
a noble work. The theatre enables us to woo
forgetfulness of self successfully for a few
brief hours, and I have seen the time when
an hour or two of relief from actual cares
has resulted in great good. Nevertheless,
the gentleman is not elected ; and if Mrs.

Pedagog will kindly refill my cup, I will ask you to join me in draining a toast to the health of the pastor of this flock, whose conscience, paradoxical as it may seem, is the most frequently worn and yet the least threadbare of the consciences represented at this table."

This easy settlement of her difficulty was so pleasing to Mrs. Pedagog that the Idiot's request was graciously acceded to, and Mr. Whitechoker's health was drank in coffee, after which the Idiot requested the genial gentleman who occasionally imbibed to join him privately in eating buckwheat cakes to the health of Mr. Davenport.

"I haven't any doubt that he is worthy of the attention," he said; "and if you will lend me the money to buy the tickets, I'll take you around to the Criterion to-night, where he is playing. I don't know whether he plays Hamlet or A Hole in the Roof; but, at any rate, we can have a good time between the acts."

IV

"I see the men are at work on the pavements this morning," said the School-Master, gazing out through the window at a number of laborers at work in the street.

"Yes," said the Idiot, calmly, "and I think Mrs. Pedagog ought to sue the Department of Public Works for libel. If she hasn't a case no maligned person ever had."

"What are you saying, sir?" queried the landlady, innocently.

"I say," returned the Idiot, pointing out into the street, "that you ought to sue the Department of Public Works for libel. They've got their sign right up against your house. *No Thorough Fare* is what it says. That's libel, isn't it, Mr. Brief?"

"It is certainly a fatal criticism of a boarding-house," observed Mr. Brief, with a twinkle in his eye, "but Mrs. Pedagog could hardly secure damages on that score."

"I don't know about that," returned the Idiot. "As I understand it, it is an old maxim of the law that the greater the truth the greater the libel. Mrs. Pedagog ought to receive a million— By-the-way, what have we this morning?"

"We have steak and fried potatoes, sir," replied Mrs. Pedagog, frigidly. "And I desire to add, that one who criticises the table as much as you do would do well to get his meals outside."

"That, Mrs. Pedagog, is not the point. The difficulty I find here lies in getting my meals inside," said the Idiot.

"Mary, you may bring in the mush," observed Mrs. Pedagog, pursing her lips, as she always did when she wished to show that she was offended.

"Yes, Mary," put in the School-Master; "let us have the mush as quickly as possible —and may it not be quite such mushy mush as the remarks we have just been favored with by our talented friend the Idiot."

"You overwhelm me with your compliments, Mr. Pedagog," replied the Idiot, cheerfully. "A flatterer like you should live in a flat."

"Has your friend completed his article on

"HAS YOUR FRIEND COMPLETED HIS ARTICLE ON OLD JOKES?"

old jokes yet?" queried the Bibliomaniac,
with a smile and some apparent irrelevance.

"Yes and no," said the Idiot. "He has
completed his labors on it by giving it up.
He is a very thorough sort of a fellow, and
he intended to make the article comprehensive, but he found he couldn't, because, judging from comments of men like you, for instance, he was forced to conclude that there
never was a *new* joke. But, as I was saying
the other morning—"

"Do you really remember what you say?"
sneered Mr. Pedagog. "You must have a
great memory for trifles."

"Sir, I shall never forget you," said the
Idiot. "But to revert to what I was saying
the other morning, I'd like to begin life all
over again, so that I could prepare myself
for the profession of architecture. It's the
greatest profession in the world, and one
which is surest to bring immortality to its
successful follower. A man may write a
splendid book, and become a great man for a
while and within certain limits, but the chances
are that some other man will come along
later and supplant him. Then the book's sale
will die out after a time, and with this will
come a diminution of its author's reputa-

tion, in extent anyway. An actor or a great preacher becomes only a name after his death, but the architect who builds a cathedral or a fine public building really erects a monument to his own memory."

"He does if he can build it so that it will stay up," said the Bibliomaniac. "I think you, however, are better off as you are. If you had a more extended reputation or a lasting name you would probably be locked up in some retreat; or if you were not, posterity would want to know why."

"I am locked up in a retreat of Nature's making," said the Idiot, with a sigh. "Nature has set around me certain limitations which, while they are not material, might as well be so as far as my ability to soar above them is concerned—and it's well she has. If it were otherwise, my life would not be safe or bearable in this company. As it is, I am happy and not at all afraid of the effects your jealousy of me might entail if I were any better than the rest of you."

"I like that," said Mr. Pedagog.

"I thought you would," said the Idiot. "That's why I said it. I aim to please, and for once seem to have hit the bull's-eye. Mary, kindly break open this biscuit for me."

"Have you ideas on the subject of architecture that you so desire to become an architect?" queried Mr. Whitechoker, who was always full of sympathy for aspiring natures.

"A few," said the Idiot.

Mr. Pedagog laughed outright.

"Let's test his ideas," he said, in an amused way. "Take a cathedral, for instance. Suppose, Mr. Idiot, a man should come to you and say: 'Idiot, we have a fund of $800,000 in our hands, actual cash. We think of building a cathedral, and we think of employing you to draw up our plans. Give us some idea of what we should do.' Do you mean to tell me that you could say anything reasonable or intelligent to that man?"

"Well, that depends upon what you call reasonable and intelligent. I have never been able to find out what you mean by those terms," the Idiot answered, slowly. "But I could tell him something that I consider reasonable and intelligent."

"From your own point of view, then, as to reasonableness and intelligence, what should you say to him?"

"I'd make him out a plan providing for the investment of his $800,000 in five-per-

cent. gold bonds, which would bring him in
an income of $40,000 a year ; after which
I should call his attention to the fact that
$40,000 a year would enable him to take 10,-
000 poor children out of this sweltering city
into the country, to romp and drink fresh
milk and eat wholesome food for two weeks
every summer from now until the end of time,
which would build up a human structure that
might be of more benefit to the world than
any pile of bricks, marble, and wrought-iron
I or any other architect could conceive of,"
said the Idiot. "The structure would stand
up, too."

"You call that architecture, do you ?" said
Mr. Pedagog.

"Yes," said the Idiot, "of the renaissance
order. But that, of course, you term idiocy — and maybe it is. I like to be that
kind of an idiot. I do not claim to be able
to build a cathedral, however. I don't suppose I could even build a boarding-house like
this, but what I should like to do in architecture would be to put up a $5000 dwelling-
house for $5000. That's a thing that has
never been done, and I think I might be able
to do it. If I did, I'd patent the plan and
make a fortune. Then I should like to know

enough about the science of planning a building to find out whether my model hotel is
practicable or not."

"You have a model hotel in your mind,
eh?" said the Bibliomaniac.

"It must be a very small hotel if it's in his
mind," said the Doctor.

"That's tantamount to saying that it isn't
anywhere," said Mr. Pedagog.

"Well, it's a great hotel just the same,"
said the Idiot. "Although I presume it would
be expensive to build. It would have movable rooms, in the first place. Each room
would be constructed like an elevator, with
appliances at hand for moving it up and
down. The great thing about this would be
that persons could have a room on any floor
they wanted it, so long as they got the room
in the beginning. A second advantage would
lie in the fact, that if you were sleeping in a
room next door to another in which there was
a crying baby, you could pull the rope and
go up two or three flights until you were free
from the noise. Then in case of fire the room
in which the fire started could be lowered
into a sliding tank large enough to immerse
the whole thing in, which I should have constructed in the cellar. If the whole building

were to catch fire, there would be no loss of life, because all the rooms could be lowered to the ground-floor, and the occupants could step right out upon solid ground. Then again, if you were down on the ground-floor, and desired to get an extended view of the surrounding country, it would be easy to raise your room to the desired elevation. Why, there's no end to the advantages to be gained from such an arrangement."

"It's a fine idea," said Mr. Pedagog, "and one worthy of your mammoth intellect. It couldn't possibly cost more than a million of dollars to erect such a hotel, could it?"

"No," said the Idiot. "And that is cheap alongside some of the hotels they are putting up nowadays."

"It could be built on less than four hundred acres of ground, too, I presume?" said the Bibliomaniac, with a wink at the Doctor.

"Certainly," said the Idiot, meekly.

"And if anybody fell sick in one of the rooms," said the Doctor, "and needed a change of air, you could have a tower over each, I suppose, so that the room could be elevated high enough to secure the different quality in the ether?"

"Undoubtedly," said the Idiot. "Although

THEY DEPARTED

that would add materially to the expense. A scarlet-fever patient, however, in a hotel like that could very easily be isolated from the rest of the house by the maintenance of what might be called the hospital floor."

"Superb!" said the Doctor. "I wonder you haven't spoken to some architectural friend about it."

"I have," said the Idiot. "You must remember that young fellow with a black mustache I had here to dinner last Saturday night."

"Yes, I remember him," said the Doctor. "Is he an architect?"

"He is—and a good one. He can take a brown-stone dwelling and turn it into a colonial mansion with a pot of yellow paint. He's a wonder. I submitted the idea to him."

"And what was his verdict?"

"I don't like to say," said the Idiot, blushing a little.

"Ha! ha!" laughed Mr. Pedagog. "I shouldn't think you would like to say. I guess we know what he said."

"I doubt it," said the Idiot; "but if you guess right, I'll tell you."

"He said you had better go and live in a

lunatic asylum," said Mr. Pedagog, with a chuckle.

"Not he," returned the Idiot, nibbling at his biscuit. "On the contrary. He advised me to stop living in one. He said contact with the rest of you was affecting my brain."

This time Mr. Pedagog did not laugh, but mistaking his coffee-cup for a piece of toast, bit a small section out of its rim ; and in the midst of Mrs. Pedagog's expostulation, which followed the School-Master's careless error, the Idiot and the Genial Old Gentleman departed, with smiles on their faces which were almost visible at the back of their respective necks.

V

"HULLO!" said the Idiot, as he began his breakfast. "This isn't Friday morning, is it? I thought it was Tuesday."

"So it is Tuesday," put in the School-Master.

"Then this fish is a little extra treat, is it?" observed the Idiot, turning with a smile to the landlady.

"Fish? That isn't fish, sir," returned the good lady. "That is liver."

"Oh, is it?" said the Idiot, apologetically. "Excuse me, my dear Mrs. Pedagog. I thought from its resistance that it was fried sole. Have you a hatchet handy?" he added, turning to the maid.

"My piece is tender enough. I can't see what you want," said the School-Master, coldly.

"I'd like your piece," replied the Idiot, suavely. "That is, if it really is tender enough."

"Don't pay any attention to him, my dear," said the School-Master to the landlady, whose ire was so very much aroused that she was about to make known her sentiments on certain subjects.

"No, Mrs. Pedagog," said the Idiot, "don't pay any attention to me, I beg of you. Anything that could add to the jealousy of Mr. Pedagog would redound to the discomfort of all of us. Besides, I really do not object to the liver. I need not eat it. And as for staying my appetite, I always stop on my way down-town after breakfast for a bite or two anyhow."

There was silence for a moment.

"I wonder why it is," began the Idiot, after tasting his coffee—"I wonder why it is Friday is fish-day all over the world, anyhow? Do you happen to be learned enough in piscatorial science to enlighten me on that point, Doctor?"

"No," returned the physician, gruffly. "I've never looked into the matter."

"I guess it's because Friday is an unlucky day," said the Idiot. "Just think of all the unlucky things that may happen before and after eating fish, as well as during the process. In the first place, before eating, you go off and fish all day, and have no luck—

"YOU FISH ALL DAY, AND HAVE NO LUCK"

don't catch a thing. You fall in the water perhaps, and lose your watch, or your fish-hook catches in your coat-tails, with the result that you come near casting yourself instead of the fly into the brook or the pond, as the case may be. Perhaps the hook doesn't stop with the coat-tails, but goes on in, and catches you. That's awfully unlucky, especially when the hook is made of unusually barby barbed wire.

"Then, again, you may go fishing on somebody else's preserves, and get arrested, and sent to jail overnight, and hauled up the next morning, and have to pay ten dollars fine for poaching. Think of Mr. Pedagog being fined ten dollars for poaching! Awfully unfortunate!"

"Kindly leave me out of your calculations," returned Mr. Pedagog, with a flush of indignation.

"Certainly, if you wish it," said the Idiot. "We'll hand Mr. Brief over to the police, and let *him* be fined for poaching on somebody else's preserves—although that's sort of impossible, too, because Mrs. Pedagog never lets us see preserves of any kind."

"We had brandied peaches last Sunday night," said the landlady, indignantly.

"Oh yes, so we did," returned the Idiot. "That must have been what the Bibliomaniac had taken," he added, turning to the genial gentleman who occasionally imbibed. "You know, we thought he'd been—ah—he'd been absorbing."

"To what do you refer?" asked the Bibliomaniac, curtly.

"To the brandied peaches," returned the Idiot. "Do not press me further, please, because we like you, old fellow, and I don't believe anybody noticed it but ourselves."

"Noticed what? I want to know what you noticed and when you noticed it," said the Bibliomaniac, savagely. "I don't want any nonsense, either. I just want a plain statement of facts. What did you notice?"

"Well, if you must have it," said the Idiot, slowly, "my friend who imbibes and I were rather pained on Sunday night to observe that you—that you had evidently taken something rather stronger than cold water, tea, or Mr. Pedagog's opinions."

"It's a libel, sir!—a gross libel!" retorted the Bibliomaniac. "How did I show it? That's what I want to know. How—did—I —show—it? Speak up quick, and loud too. How did I show it?"

HE COULD BE HEARD THROWING THINGS ABOUT

"Well, you went up-stairs after tea."

"Yes, sir, I did."

"And my friend who imbibes and I were left down in the front hall, and while we were talking there you put your head over the banisters and asked, 'Who's that down there?' Remember that?"

"Yes, sir, I do. And you replied, ' Mr. Auburnose and myself.'"

"Yes. And then you asked, ' Who are the other two?'"

"Well, I did. What of it?"

"Mr. Auburnose and I were there alone. That's what of it. Now I put a charitable construction on the matter and say it was the peaches, when you fly off the handle like one of Mrs. Pedagog's coffee-cups."

"Sir!" roared the Bibliomaniac, jumping from his chair. "You are the greatest idiot I know."

"Sir!" returned the Idiot, "you flatter me."

But the Bibliomaniac was not there to hear. He had rushed from the room, and during the deep silence that ensued he could be heard throwing things about in the chamber overhead, and in a very few moments the banging of the front door and scurrying down the brown - stone steps showed that he had gone out of doors to cool off.

"It is too bad," said the Idiot, after a while, "that he has such a quick temper. It doesn't do a bit of good to get mad that way. He'll be uncomfortable all day long, and over what? Just because I attempted to say a good word for him, and announce the restoration of my confidence in his temperance qualities, he cuts up a high-jinks that makes everybody uncomfortable.

"But to resume about this fish business," continued the Idiot. "Fish—"

"Oh, fish be hanged!" said the Doctor, impatiently. "We've had enough of fish."

"Very well," returned the idiot; "as you wish. Hanging isn't the best treatment for fish, but we'll let that go. I never cared for the finny tribe myself, and if Mrs. Pedagog can be induced to do it, I for one am in favor of keeping shad, shark, and shrimps out of the house altogether."

VI

THE Idiot was unusually thoughtful—a fact which made the School-Master and the Bibliomaniac unusually nervous. Their stock criticism of him was that he was thoughtless; and yet when he so far forgot his natural propensities as to meditate, they did not like it. It made them uneasy. They had a haunting fear that he was conspiring with himself against them, and no man, not even a callous school-master or a confirmed bibliomaniac, enjoys feeling that he is the object of a conspiracy. The thing to do, then, upon this occasion, seemed obviously to interrupt his train of thought—to put obstructions upon his mental track, as it were, and ditch the express, which they feared was getting up steam at that moment to run them down.

"You don't seem quite yourself this morning, sir," said the Bibliomaniac.

"Don't I?" queried the Idiot. "And whom do I seem to be?"

"I mean that you seem to have something on your mind that worries you," said the Bibliomaniac.

"No, I haven't anything on my mind," returned the Idiot. "I was thinking about you and Mr. Pedagog—which implies a thought not likely to use up much of my gray matter."

"Do you think your head holds any gray matter?" put in the Doctor.

"Rather verdant, I should say," said Mr. Pedagog.

"Green, gray, or pink," said the Idiot, "choose your color. It does not affect the fact that I was thinking about the Bibliomaniac and Mr. Pedagog. I have a great scheme in hand, which only requires capital and the assistance of those two gentlemen to launch it on the sea of prosperity. If any of you gentlemen want to get rich and die in comfort as the owner of your homes, now is your chance."

"In what particular line of business is your scheme?" asked Mr. Whitechoker. He had often felt that he would like to die in comfort, and to own a little house, even if it had a large mortgage on it.

"Journalism," said the Idiot. "There is a pile of money to be made out of journalism, particularly if you happen to strike a new idea. Ideas count."

"How far up do your ideas count—up to five?" questioned Mr. Pedagog, with a tinge of sarcasm in his tone.

"I don't know about that," returned the Idiot. "The idea I have hold of now, however, will count up into the millions if it can only be set going, and before each one of those millions will stand a big capital S with two black lines drawn vertically through it —in other words, my idea holds dollars, but to get the crop you've got to sow the seed. Plant a thousand dollars in my idea, and next year you'll reap two thousand. Plant that, and next year you'll have four thousand, and so on. At that rate millions come easy."

"I'll give you a dollar for the idea," said the Bibliomaniac.

"No, I don't want to sell. You'll do to help develop the scheme. You'll make a first-rate tool, but you aren't the workman to manage the tool. I will go as far as to say, however, that without you and Mr. Pedagog, or your equivalents in the animal kingdom, the idea isn't worth the fabulous sum you offer."

"You have quite aroused my interest," said Mr. Whitechoker. "Do you propose to start a new paper?"

"You are a good guesser," replied the Idiot. "That is a part of the scheme—but it isn't the idea. I propose to start a new paper in accordance with the plan which the idea contains."

"Is it to be a magazine, or a comic paper, or what?" asked the Bibliomaniac.

"Neither. It's a daily."

"That's nonsense," said Mr. Pedagog, putting his spoon into the condensed-milk can by mistake. "There isn't a single scheme in daily journalism that hasn't been tried—except printing an evening paper in the morning."

"That's been tried," said the Idiot. "I know of an evening paper the second edition of which is published at mid-day. That's an old dodge, and there's money in it, too— money that will never be got out of it. But I really have a grand scheme. So many of our dailies, you know, go in for every horrid detail of daily events that people are beginning to tire of them. They contain practical-

"HE WAS NOT MURDERED"

ly the same things day after day. So many
columns of murder, so many beautiful sui-
cides, so much sport, a modicum of general
intelligence, plenty of fires, no end of embez-
zlements, financial news, advertisements, and
head-lines. Events, like history, repeat themselves, until people have grown weary of
them. They want something new. For instance, if you read in your morning paper
that a man has shot another man, you know
that the man who was shot was an inoffen-
sive person who never injured a soul, stood
high in the community in which he lived, and
leaves a widow with four children. On the
other hand, you know without reading the
account that the murderer shot his victim in
self-defence, and was apprehended by the de-
tectives late last night; that his counsel for-
bid him to talk to the reporters, and that it
is rumored that he comes of a good family
living in New England.

"If a breach of trust is committed, you
know that the defaulter was the last man of
whom such an act would be suspected, and,
except in the one detail of its location and
sect, that he was prominent in some church.
You can calculate to a cent how much has been
stolen by a glance at the amount of space de-

voted to the account of the crime. Loaf of
bread, two lines. Thousand dollars, ten lines.
Hundred thousand dollars, half-column. Million dollars, a full column. Five million dollars, half the front page, wood-cut of the em-
bezzler, and two editorials, one leader and one
paragraph.

"And so with everything. We are creat-
ures of habit. The expected always happens,
and newspapers are dull because the events
they chronicle are dull."

"Granting the truth of this," put in the
School - Master, "what do you propose to
do?"

"Get up a newspaper that will devote its
space to telling what hasn't happened."

"That's been done," said the Bibliomaniac.

"To a much more limited extent than we
think," returned the Idiot. "It has never
been done consistently and truthfully."

"I fail to see how a newspaper can be
made to prevaricate truthfully," asserted Mr.
Whitechoker. To tell the truth, he was greatly disappointed with the idea, because he
could not in the nature of things become one
of its beneficiaries.

"I haven't suggested prevarication," said
the Idiot. "Put on your front page, for in-

"SUPERINTENDENT SMITHERS HAS NOT ABSCONDED"

stance, an item like this : 'George Bronson, colored, aged twenty - nine, a resident of Thompson Street, was caught cheating at poker last night. He was not murdered.' There you tell what has not happened. There is a variety about it. It has the charm of the unexpected. Then you might say : 'Curious incident on Wall Street yesterday. So-and-so, who was caught on the bear side of the market with 10,000 shares of J. B. & S. K. W., paid off all his obligations in full, and retired from business with $1,000,000 clear.' Or we might say, 'Superintendent Smithers, of the St. Goliath's Sunday-school, who is also cashier in the Forty-eighth National Bank, has not absconded with $4,000,000.'"

"Oh, that's a rich idea," put in the School-Master. "You'd earn $1,000,000 in libel suits the first year."

"No, you wouldn't, either," said the Idiot. "You don't libel a man when you say he hasn't murdered anybody. Quite the contrary, you call attention to his conspicuous virtue. You are in reality commending those who refrain from criminal practice, instead of delighting those who are fond of departing from the paths of Christianity by giving them notoriety."

"But I fail to see in what respect Mr. Pedagog and I are essential to your scheme," said the Bibliomaniac.

"I must confess to some curiosity on my own part on that point," added the School-Master.

"Why, it's perfectly clear," returned the Idiot, with a conciliating smile as he prepared to depart. "You both know so much that isn't so, that I rather rely on you to fill up."

VII

A NEW boarder had joined the circle about
Mrs. Pedagog's breakfast-table. He had
what the Idiot called a three-ply name—
which was Richard Henderson Warren—and
he was by profession a poet. Whether it was
this that made it necessary for him to board
or not, the rewards of the muse being rather
slender, was known only to himself, and he
showed no disposition to enlighten his fellow-boarders on the subject. His success as a
poet Mrs. Pedagog found it hard to gauge;
for while the postman left almost daily nu-
merous letters, the envelopes of which showed
that they came from the various periodicals
of the day, it was never exactly clear whether
or not the missives contained remittances or
rejected manuscripts, though the fact that
Mr. Warren was the only boarder in the
house who had requested to have a waste-
basket added to the furniture of his room

seemed to indicate that they contained the latter. To this request Mrs. Pedagog had gladly acceded, because she had a notion that therein at some time or another would be found a clew to the new boarder's past history—or possibly some evidence of such duplicity as the good lady suspected he might be guilty of. She had read that Byron was profligate, and that Poe was addicted to drink, and she was impressed with the idea that poets generally were bad men, and she regarded the waste-basket as a possible means of protecting herself against any such idiosyncrasies of her new-found genius as would operate to her disadvantage if not looked after in time.

This waste-basket she made it her daily duty to empty, and in the privacy of her own room. Half-finished "ballads, songs, and snatches" she perused before consigning them to the flames or to the large jute bag in the cellar, for which the ragman called two or three times a year. Once Mrs. Pedagog's heart almost stopped beating when she found at the bottom of the basket a printed slip beginning, "*The Editor regrets that the enclosed lines are unavailable,*" and closing with about thirteen reasons, any one or all

of which might have been the main cause of
the poet's disappointment. Had it not been
for the kindly clause in the printed slip that
insinuated in graceful terms that this rejec-
tion did not imply a lack of literary merit
in the contribution itself, the good lady,
knowing well that there was even less money
to be made from rejected than from accept-
ed poetry, would have been inclined to request the poet to vacate the premises. The
very next day, however, she was glad she
had not requested the resignation of the poet
from the laureateship of her house ; for the
same basket gave forth another printed slip
from another editor, begging the poet to
accept the enclosed check, with thanks for
his contribution, and asking him to de-
posit it as soon as practicable — which
was pleasing enough, since it implied
that the poet was the possessor of a bank
account.

Now Mrs. Pedagog was consumed with curiosity to know for how large a sum the check
called—which desire was gratified a few days
later, when the inspired boarder paid his
week's bill with three one-dollar bills and a
check, signed by a well-known publisher, for
two dollars.

By the boarders themselves the poet was regarded with much interest. The School-Master had read one or two of his effusions in the Fireside Corner of the journal he received weekly from his home up in New England—effusions which showed no little merit, as well as indicating that Mr. Warren wrote for a literary syndicate ; Mr. White-choker had known of him as the young man who was to have written a Christmas carol for his Sunday-school a year before, and who had finished and presented the manuscript shortly after New-Year's day ; while to the Idiot, Mr. Warren's name was familiar as that of a frequent contributor to the funny papers of the day.

"I was very much amused by your poem in the last number of the *Observer*, Mr. Warren," said the Idiot, as they sat down to breakfast together.

"Were you, indeed ?" returned Mr. Warren. "I am sorry to hear that, for it was intended to be a serious effort."

"Of course it was, Mr. Warren, and so it appeared," said the School-Master, with an indignant glance at the Idiot. "It was a very dignified and stately bit of work, and I must congratulate you upon it."

THE INSPIRED BOARDER PAID HIS BILL

"I didn't mean to give offence," said the Idiot. "I've read so much of yours that was purely humorous that I believe I'd laugh at a dirge if you should write one ; but I really thought your lines in the *Observer* were a burlesque. You had the same thought that Rossetti expresses in 'The Woodspurge':

> 'The wind flapped loose, the wind was still,
> Shaken out dead from tree to hill ;
> I had walked on at the wind's will,
> I sat now, for the wind was still.'

That's Rossetti, if you remember. Slightly suggestive of 'Blow Ye Winds of the Morning! Blow! Blow! Blow!' but more or less pleasing."

"I recall the poem you speak of," said Warren, with dignity ; "but the true poet, sir—and I hope I have some claim to be considered as such—never so far forgets himself as to burlesque his masters."

"Well, I don't know what to call it, then, when a poet takes the same thought that has previously been used by his masters and makes a funny poem—"

"But," returned the Poet, warmly, "it was not a funny poem."

"It made me laugh," retorted the Idiot,

" and that is more than half the professedly
funny poems we get nowadays can do. Therefore I say it was a funny poem, and I don't
see how you can deny that it was a burlesque
of Rossetti."

" Well, I do deny it *in toto.*"

" I don't know anything about denying it
in toto," rejoined the Idiot, " but I'd deny it
in print if I were you. I know plenty of
people who think it was a burlesque, and I
overheard one man say — he is a Rossetti
crank — that you ought to be ashamed of
yourself for writing it."

" There is no use of discussing the matter
further," said the Poet. " I am innocent of
any such intent as you have ascribed to me,
and if people say I have burlesqued Rossetti
they say what is not true."

" Did you ever read that little poem of
Swinburne's called ' The Boy at the Gate ' ?"
asked the Idiot, to change the subject.

" I have no recollection of it," said the Poet,
shortly.

" The name sounds familiar," put in Mr.
Whitechoker, anxious not to be left out of a
literary discussion.

" I have read it, but I forget just how it
goes," vouchsafed the School-Master, forget-

ting for a moment the Robert Elsmere ep-
isode and its lesson.

"It goes something like this," said the
Idiot:

"Sombre and sere the slim sycamore sighs;
Lushly the lithe leaves lie low o'er the land;
Whistles the wind with its whisperings wise,
Grewsomely gloomy and garishly grand.
So doth the sycamore solemnly stand,
Wearily watching in wondering wait;
So it has stood for six centuries, and
Still it is waiting the boy at the gate."

"No; I never read the poem," said Mr.
Whitechoker, "but I'd know it was Swinburne in a minute. He has such a command
of alliterative language."

"Yes," said the Poet, with an uneasy glance
at the Idiot. "It is Swinburnian; but what
was the poem about?"

"'The boy at the gate,'" said the Idiot.
"The idea was that the sycamore was standing there for centuries waiting for the boy
who never turns up."

"It really is a beautiful thought," put in
Mr. Whitechoker. "It is, I presume, an alle-
gory to contrast faithful devotion and con-
stancy with unfaithfulness and fickleness.

Such thoughts occur only to the wholly gifted. It is only to the poetic temperament that the conception of such a thought can come coupled with the ability to voice it in fitting terms. There is a grandeur about the lines the Idiot has quoted that betrays the master-mind."

"Very true," said the School-Master, "and I take this opportunity to say that I am most agreeably surprised in the Idiot. It is no small thing even to be able to repeat a poet's lines so carefully, and with so great lucidity, and so accurately, as I can testify that he has just done."

"Don't be too pleased, Mr. Pedagog," said the Idiot, dryly. "I only wanted to show Mr. Warren that you and Mr. White-choker, mines of information though you are, have not as yet worked up a corner on knowledge to the exclusion of the rest of us." And with these words the Idiot left the table.

"He is a queer fellow," said the School-Master. "He is full of pretence and hollowness, but he is sometimes almost brilliant."

"What you say is very true," said Mr. Whitechoker. "I think he has just escaped

"I KNOW YOU CAN'T, BECAUSE IT ISN'T THERE"

being a smart man. I wish we could take
him in hand, Mr. Pedagog, and make him
more of a fellow than he is."

Later in the day the Poet met the Idiot on
the stairs. "I say," he said, "I've looked all
through Swinburne, and I can't find that
poem."

"I know you can't," returned the Idiot, "because it isn't there. Swinburne never wrote
it. It was a little thing of my own. I was
only trying to get a rise out of Mr. Pedagog
and his Reverence with it. You have frequently appeared impressed by the undoubtedly impressive manner of these two gentlemen. I wanted to show you what their
opinions were worth."

"Thank you," returned the Poet, with a
smile. "Don't you want to go into partnership with me and write for the funny papers?
It would be a splendid thing for me—your
ideas are so original."

"And I can see fun in everything, too,"
said the Idiot, thoughtfully.

"Yes," returned the Poet. "Even in my
serious poems."

Which remark made the Idiot blush a little, but he soon recovered his composure and
made a firm friend of the Poet.

The first fruits of the partnership have not yet appeared, however.

As for Messrs. Whitechoker and Pedagog, when they learned how they had been deceived, they were so indignant that they did not speak to the Idiot for a week.

VIII

It was Sunday morning, and Mr. Whitechoker, as was his wont on the first day of
the week, appeared at the breakfast table severe as to his mien.

"Working on Sunday weighs on his mind,"
the Idiot said to the Bibliomaniac, "but I
don't see why it should. The luxury of rest
that he allows himself the other six days of
the week is surely an atonement for the hours
of labor he puts in on Sunday."

But it was not this that on Sunday mornings weighed on the mind of the Reverend
Mr. Whitechoker. He appeared more serious
of visage then because he had begun to think
of late that his fellow-boarders lived too
much in the present, and ignored almost to-
tally that which might be expected to come.
He had been revolving in his mind for several weeks the question as to whether it was or
was not his Christian duty to attempt to in-

fluence the lives of these men with whom the chances of life had brought him in contact. He had finally settled it to his own satisfaction that it was his duty so to do, and he had resolved, as far as lay in his power, to direct the conversation at Sunday morning's breakfast into spiritual rather than into temporal matters.

So, as Mrs. Pedagog was pouring the coffee, Mr. Whitechoker began :

"Do you gentlemen ever pause in your every-day labors and thought to let your minds rest upon the future — the possibilities it has in store for us, the consequences which—"

"No mush, thank you," said the Idiot. Then turning to Mr. Whitechoker, he added : "I can't answer for the other gentlemen at this board, but I can assure you, Mr. Whitechoker, that I often do so. It was only last night, sir, that my genial friend who imbibes and I were discussing the future and its possibilities, and I venture to assert that there is no more profitable food for reflection anywhere in the larders of the mind than that."

"Larders of the mind is excellent," said the School-Master, with a touch of sarcasm in his voice. "Perhaps you would not mind opening the door to your mental pantry, and letting us peep within at the stores you keep there. I am sure that on the subject in hand your views cannot fail to be original as well as edifying."

"I am also sure," said Mr. Whitechoker, somewhat surprised to hear the Idiot speak as he did, having sometimes ventured to doubt if that flippant-minded young man ever reflected on the serious side of life—"I am also sure that it is most gratifying to hear that you have done some thinking on the subject."

"I am glad you are gratified, Mr. Whitechoker," replied the Idiot, "but I am far from taking undue credit to myself because I reflect upon the future and its possibilities. I do not see how any man can fail to be interested in the subject, particularly when he considers the great strides science has made in the last twenty years."

"I fail to see," said the School-Master, "what the strides of science have to do with it."

"You fail to see so often, Mr. Pedagog," returned the Idiot, "that I would advise your eyes to make an assignment in favor of your pupils."

"I must confess," put in Mr. Whitechoker, blandly, "that I too am somewhat—er—somewhat—"

"Somewhat up a tree as to science's connection with the future?" queried the Idiot.

"You have my meaning, but hardly the phraseology I should have chosen," replied the minister.

"My style is rather epigrammatic," said the Idiot, suavely. "I appreciate the flattery implied by your noticing it. But science has everything to do with it. It is science that is going to make the future great. It is science that has annihilated distance, and the annihilation has just begun. Twenty years ago it was hardly possible for a man standing on one side of the street to make himself heard on the other, the acoustic properties of the atmosphere not being what they should be. To-day you can stand in the pulpit of your church, and by means of certain scientific apparatus make yourself heard in Boston, New Orleans, or San Francisco. Has this no bearing on the future? The time will come, Mr. Whitechoker, when your missionaries will be able to sit in their comfortable rectories, and ring up the heathen in foreign climes, and convert them over the telephone, without run-

" YOU CAN MAKE YOURSELF HEARD IN SAN FRANCISCO "

ning the slightest danger of falling into the soup, which expression I use in its literal rather than in its metaphorical sense."

" But—" interrupted Mr. Whitechoker.

" Now wait, please," said the Idiot. "If science can annihilate degrees of distance, who shall say that before many days science may not annihilate degrees of time? If San Francisco, thousands of miles distant, can be brought within range of the ear, why cannot 1990 be brought before the mind's eye? And if 1990 can be brought before the mind's eye, what is to prevent the invention of a prophetograph which shall enable us to cast a horoscope which shall reach all around eternity and half-way back, if not further?"

" You do not understand me," said Mr. Whitechoker. " When I speak of the future, I do not mean the temporal future."

" I know exactly what you mean," said the Idiot. " I've dealt in futures, and I am familiar with all kinds. It is you, sir, that do not understand me. My claim is perfectly plausible, and in its results is bound to make the world better. Do you suppose that any man who, by the aid of my prophetograph, sees that on a certain date in the future he will be hanged for murder is going to fail to provide himself with an alibi in regard to that particular murder, and must we not admit that having provided himself with that alibi he will of necessity avoid bloodshed, and so avoid the gallows? That's reasonable. So in regard to all the thousand and one other peccadilloes that go to make this life a sinful one. Science, by a purely logical advance along the lines already mapped out for itself, and in part already traversed, will enable men to avoid the pitfalls and reap only the windfalls of life ; we shall all see what terrible consequences await on a single misstep, and we shall not make the misstep. Can you still claim that science and the future have nothing to do with each other?"

"You are talking of matters purely temporal," said Mr. Whitechoker. "I have reference to our spiritual future."

"And the two," observed the Idiot, "are so closely allied that we cannot separate them. The proverb about looking after the pennies and letting the pounds take care of themselves applies here. I believe that if I take care of my temporal future — which, by-the-way, does not exist—my spiritual future will take care of itself; and if science places the hereafter before us—and you admit that even

THE PROPHETOGRAPH

now it is before us — all we have to do is to
take advantage of our opportunities, and mend
our lives accordingly."

"But if science shows you what is to come,"
said the School-Master, "it must show your fate
with perfect accuracy, or it ceases to be science,
in which event your entertaining notions as
to reform and so on are entirely fallacious."

"Not at all," said the Idiot. "We are ap-
proaching the time when science, which is
much more liberal than any other branch of
knowledge, will sacrifice even truth itself for
the good of mankind."

"You ought to start a paradox company,"
suggested the Doctor.

"Either that or make himself the nucleus
of an insane asylum," observed the School-
Master, viciously. "I never knew a man with
such maniacal views as those we have heard
this morning."

"There is a great deal, Mr. Pedagog, that
you have never known," returned the Idiot.
"Stick by me, and you'll die with a mind
richly stored."

Whereat the School-Master left the table
with such manifest impatience that Mr. Whitechoker was sorry he had started the conversation.

The genial gentleman who occasionally imbibed and the Idiot withdrew to the latter's room, where the former observed:

"What are you driving at, anyhow? Where did you get those crazy ideas?"

"I ate a Welsh-rarebit last night, and dreamed 'em," returned the Idiot.

"I thought as much," said his companion. "What deuced fine things dreams are, anyhow!"

IX

BREAKFAST was very nearly over, and it was of such exceptionally good quality that very few remarks had been made. Finally the ball was set rolling by the Lawyer.

"How many packs of cigarettes do you smoke a day?" he asked, as the Idiot took one from his pocket and placed it at the side of his coffee-cup.

"Never more than forty-six," said the Idiot. "Why? Do you think of starting a cigarette stand?"

"Not at all," said Mr. Brief. "I was only wondering what chance you had to live to maturity, that's all. Your maturity period will be in about eight hundred and sixty years from now, the way I calculate, and it seemed to me that, judging from the number of cigarettes you smoke, you were not likely to last through more than two or three of those years."

"Oh, I expect to live longer than that," said the Idiot. "I think I'm good for at least four years. Don't you, Doctor?"

"I decline to have anything to say about your case," retorted the Doctor, whose feeling towards the Idiot was not surpassingly affectionate.

"In that event I shall probably live five years more," said the Idiot.

The Doctor's lip curled, but he remained silent.

"You'll live," put in Mr. Pedagog, with a chuckle. "The good die young."

"How did you happen to keep alive all this time then, Mr. Pedagog?" asked the Idiot.

"I have always eschewed tobacco in every form, for one thing," said Mr. Pedagog.

"I am surprised," put in the Idiot. "That's really a bad habit, and I marvel greatly that you should have done it."

The School-Master frowned, and looked at the Idiot over the rims of his glasses, as was his wont when he was intent upon getting explanations.

"Done what?" he asked, severely.

"Chewed tobacco," replied the Idiot. "You just said that one of the things that has kept you lingering in this vale of tears was that you have always chewed tobacco. I never did that, and I never shall do it, because I deem it a detestable diversion."

"I didn't say anything of the sort," retorted Mr. Pedagog, getting red in the face. "I never said that I chewed tobacco in any form."

"Oh, come!" said the Idiot, with well-feigned impatience, "what's the use of talking that way? We all heard what you said, and I have no doubt that it came as a shock to every member of this assemblage. It certainly was a shock to me, because, with all my weaknesses and bad habits, I think tobacco-chewing unutterably bad. The worst part of it is that you chew it in every form. A man who chews chewing-tobacco only may some time throw off the habit, but when one gets to be such a victim to it that he chews up cigars and cigarettes and plugs of pipe tobacco, it seems to me he is incurable. It is not only a bad habit then; it amounts to a vice."

Mr. Pedagog was getting apoplectic. "You know well enough that I never said the words you attribute to me," he said, sternly.

"Really, Mr. Pedagog," returned the Idiot,

with an irritating shake of his head, as if he were confidentially hinting to the School-Master to keep quiet—"really you pain me by these futile denials. Nobody forced you into the confession. You made it entirely of your own volition. Now I ask you, as a man and brother, what's the use of saying anything more about it? We believe you to be a person of the strictest veracity, but when you say a thing before a tableful of listeners one minute, and deny it the next, we are forced to one of two conclusions, neither of which is pleasing. We must conclude that either, repenting your confession, you sacrifice the truth, or that the habit to which you have confessed has entirely destroyed your perception of the moral question involved. Undue use of tobacco has, I believe, driven men crazy. Opium-eating has destroyed all regard for truth in one whose word had always been regarded as good as a government bond. I presume the undue use of tobacco can accomplish the same sad result. By-the-way, did you ever try opium?"

"Opium is ruin," said the Doctor, Mr. Pedagog's indignation being so great that he seemed to be unable to find the words he

was evidently desirous of hurling at the
Idiot.

"It is, indeed," said the Idiot. "I knew
a man once who smoked one little pipeful of
it, and, while under its influence, sat down at
his table and wrote a story of the supernat-
ural order that was so good that everybody
said he must have stolen it from Poe or
some other master of the weird, and now
nobody will have anything to do with
him. Tobacco, however, in the sane use of
it, is a good thing. I don't know of anything
that is more satisfying to the tired man than
to lie back on a sofa, of an evening, and puff
clouds of smoke and rings into the air. One
of the finest dreams I ever had came from
smoking. I had blown a great mountain of
smoke out into the room, and it seemed to
become real, and I climbed to its summit and
saw the most beautiful country at my feet—
a country in which all men were happy,
where there were no troubles of any kind,
where no whim was left ungratified, where
jealousies were not, and where every man
who made more than enough to live on paid
the surplus into the common treasury for the
use of those who hadn't made quite enough.
It was a national realization of the golden

rule, and I maintain that if smoking were bad nothing so good, even in the abstract form of an idea, could come out of it."

"That's a very nice thought," said the Poet. "I'd like to put that into verse. The idea of a people dividing up their surplus of wealth among the less successful strugglers is beautiful."

"You can have it," said the Idiot, with a pleased smile. "I don't write poetry of that kind myself unless I work hard, and I've found that when the poet works hard he produces poems that read hard. You are welcome to it. Another time I was dreaming over my cigar, after a day of the hardest kind of trouble at the office. Everything had gone wrong with me, and I was blue as indigo. I came home here, lit a cigar, and threw myself down upon my bed and began to puff. I felt like a man in a deep pit, out of which there was no way of getting. I closed my eyes for a second, and to all intents and purposes I lay in that pit. And then what did tobacco do for me? Why, it lifted me right out of my prison. I thought I was sitting on a rock down in the depths. The stars twinkled tantalizingly above me. They invited me to freedom, knowing that freedom

"I GRASPED IT IN MY TWO HANDS"

was not attainable. Then I blew a ring of smoke from my mouth, and it began to rise slowly at first, and then, catching in a current of air, it flew upward more rapidly, widening constantly, until it disappeared in the darkness above. Then I had a thought. I filled my mouth as full of smoke as possible, and blew forth the greatest ring you ever saw, and as it started to rise I grasped it in my two hands. It struggled beneath my weight, lengthened out into an elliptical link, and broke, and let me down with a dull thud. Then I made two rings, grasping one with my left hand and the other with my right—"

"And they lifted you out of the pit, I suppose?" sneered the Bibliomaniac.

"I do not say that they did," said the Idiot, calmly. "But I do know that when I opened my eyes I wasn't in the pit any longer, but up-stairs in my hall-bedroom."

"How awfully mysterious!" said the Doctor, satirically.

"Well, I don't approve of smoking," said Mr. Whitechoker. "I agree with the London divine who says it is the pastime of perdition. It is not prompted by natural instincts. It is only the habit of artificial civilization. Dogs and horses and birds get along without it. Why shouldn't man?"

"Hear! hear!" cried Mr. Pedagog, clapping his hands approvingly.

"Where? where?" put in the Idiot. "That's a great argument. Dog's don't put up in boarding-houses. Is the boarding-house, therefore, the result of a degraded, artificial civilization? I have seen educated horses that didn't smoke, but I have never seen an educated horse, or an uneducated one, for that matter, that had even had the chance to smoke, or the kind of mouth that would enable him to do it in case he had the chance. I have also observed that horses don't read books, that birds don't eat mutton-chops, that dogs don't go to the opera, that donkeys don't play the piano—at least, four-legged donkeys don't—so you might as well argue that since horses, dogs, birds, and donkeys get along without literature, music, mutton-chops, and piano-playing—"

"You've covered music," put in the Lawyer, who liked to be precise.

"True; but piano-playing isn't always music," returned the Idiot. "You might as well argue because the beasts and the birds do without these things man ought to. Fish don't smoke, neither do they join the police-force, therefore man should nei-

" PIANO-PLAYING ISN'T ALWAYS MUSIC "

ther smoke nor become a guardian of the peace."

"Nevertheless it is a pastime of perdition," insisted Mr. Whitechoker.

"No, it isn't," retorted the Idiot. "Smoking is the business of perdition. It smokes because it has to."

"There! there!" remonstrated Mr. Pedagog.

"You mean hear! hear! I presume," said the Idiot.

"I mean that you have said enough!" remarked Mr. Pedagog, sharply.

"Very well," said the Idiot. "If I have convinced you all I am satisfied, not to say gratified. But really, Mr. Pedagog," he added, rising to leave the room, "if I were you I'd give up the practice of chewing—"

"Hold on a minute, Mr. Idiot," said Mr. Whitechoker, interrupting. He was desirous that Mr. Pedagog should not be further irritated. "Let me ask you one question. Does your old father smoke?"

"No," said the Idiot, leaning easily over the back of his chair—"no. What of it?"

"Nothing at all—except that perhaps if he could get along without it you might," suggested the clergyman.

"He couldn't get along without it if he knew what good tobacco was," said the Idiot.

"Then why don't you introduce him to it?" asked the Minister.

"Because I do not wish to make him unhappy," returned the Idiot, softly. "He thinks his seventy years have been the happiest years that any mortal ever had, and if now in his seventy-first year he discovered that during the whole period of his manhood he had been deprived through ignorance of so great a blessing as a good cigar, he'd become like the rest of us, living in anticipation of delights to come, and not finding approximate bliss in living over the past. Trust me, my dear Mr. Whitechoker, to look after him. He and my mother and my life are all I have."

The Idiot left the room, and Mr. Pedagog put in a greater part of the next half-hour in making personal statements to the remaining boarders to the effect that the word he used was eschewed, and not the one attributed to him by the Idiot.

Strange to say, most of them were already aware of that fact.

X

"THE progress of invention in this country has been very remarkable," said Mr. Pedagog, as he turned his attention from a scientific weekly he had been reading to a towering pile of buckwheat cakes that Mary had just brought in. "An Englishman has just discovered a means by which a ship in distress at sea can write for help on the clouds."

"Extraordinary!" said Mr. Whitechoker.

"It might be more so," observed the Idiot, coaxing the platterful of cakes out of the School-Master's reach by a dextrous movement of his hand. "And it will be more so some day. The time is coming when the moon itself will be used by some enterprising American to advertise his soap business. I haven't any doubt that the next fifty years will develop a stereopticon by means of which a picture of a certain brand of cigar may be projected through space until it seems to be held between the teeth of the man in the moon, with a printed legend below it stating that this is *Tooforfivers Best, Rolled from Hand-made Tobacco, Warranted not to Crock or Fade, and for sale by All Tobacconists at Eighteen for a Dime.*"

"You would call that an advance in invention, eh?" asked the School-Master.

"Why not?" queried the Idiot.

"Do you consider the invention which would enable man to debase nature to the level of an advertising medium an advance?"

"I should not consider the use of the moon for the dissemination of good news a debasement. If the cigars were good—and I have no doubt that some one will yet invent a cheap cigar that is good—it would benefit the human race to be acquainted with that fact. I think sometimes that the advertisements in the newspapers and the periodicals of the day are of more value to the public than the reading-matter, so-called, that stands next to them. I don't see why you should sneer at advertising. I should never have known you, for instance, Mr. Pedagog, had it not been for Mrs. Pedagog's advertisement offering board and lodging to single gentle-

"THE MOON ITSELF WILL BE USED"

men for a consideration. Nor would you have met Mrs. Smithers, now your estimable wife, yourself, had it not been for that advertisement. Why, then, do you sneer at the ladder upon which you have in a sense climbed to your present happiness? You are ungrateful."

"How you do ramify!" said Mr. Pedagog. "I believe there is no subject in the world which you cannot connect in some way or another with every other subject in the world. A discussion of the merits of Shakespeare's sonnets could be turned by your dextrous tongue in five minutes into a quarrel over the comparative merits of cider and cod-liver oil as beverages, with you, the chances are, the advocate of cod-liver oil as a steady drink."

"Well, I must say," said the Idiot, with a smile, "it has been my experience that cod-liver oil is steadier than cider. The cod-liver oils I have had the pleasure of absorbing have been evenly vile, while the ciders that I have drank have been of a variety of goodness, badness, and indifferentness which has brought me to the point where I never touch it. But to return to inventions, since you desire to limit our discussion to a single subject, I think it is about the most interesting field of speculation imaginable."

"There you are right," said Mr. Pedagog, approvingly. "There is absolutely no limit to the possibilities involved. It is almost within the range of possibilities that some man may yet invent a buckwheat cake that will satisfy your abnormal craving for that delicacy, which the present total output of this table seems unable to do."

Here Mr. Pedagog turned to his wife, and added : "My dear, will you request the cook hereafter to prepare individual cakes for us ? The Idiot has so far monopolized all that have as yet appeared."

"It appears to me," said the Idiot at this point, "that *you* are the ramifier, Mr. Pedagog. Nevertheless, ramify as much as you please. I can follow you—at a safe distance, of course — in the discussion of anything, from Edison to flapjacks. I think your suggestion regarding individual cakes is a good one. We might all have separate griddles, upon which Gladys, the cook, can prepare them, and on these griddles might be cast in bold relief the crest of each member of this household, so that every man's cake should, by an easy process in the making, come off the fire indelibly engraved with the evidence of its destiny. Mr. Pedagog's iron, for instance, might have upon it a school-book rampant, or a large head in the same condition. Mr. Whitechoker's cake-mark might be a pulpit rampant, based upon a vestryman dormant. The Doctor might have a lozengy shield with a suitable tincture, while my genial friend who occasionally imbibes could have a barry shield surmounted by a small effigy of Gambrinus."

"You appear to know something of heraldry," said the poet, with a look of surprise.

"I know something of everything," said the Idiot, complacently.

"It's a pity you don't know everything about something," sneered the Doctor.

"I would suggest," said the School-Master, dryly, "that a little rampant jackass would make a good crest for your cakes."

"That's a very good idea," said the Idiot. "I do not know but that a jackass rampant would be about as comprehensive of my virtues as anything I might select. The jackass is a combination of all the best qualities. He is determined. He minds his own business. He doesn't indulge in flippant conversation. He is useful. Has no vices, never pretends to be anything but a jackass, and most respectfully declines to be ridden by Tom, Dick, and Harry. I accept the suggestion of Mr. Pedagog with thanks. But we are still ramifying. Let us get back to inventions. Now I fully believe that the time is coming when some inventive genius will devise a method whereby intellect can be given to those who haven't any. I believe that the time is coming when the secrets of the universe will be yielded up to man by nature."

" And then ?" queried Mr. Brief.

" Then some man will try to improve on the secrets of the universe. He will try to invent an apparatus by means of which the rotation of the world may be made faster or slower, according to his will. If he has but one day, for instance, in which to do a stated piece of work, and he needs two, he will put on some patent brake and slow the world up until the distance travelled in one hour shall be reduced one-half, so that one hour under the old system will be equivalent to two ; or if he is anticipating some joy, some diversion in the future, the same smart person will find a way to increase the speed of the earth so that the hours will be like minutes. Then

"DECLINES TO BE RIDDEN"

he'll begin fooling with gravitation, and he will discover a new-fashioned lodestone, which can be carried in one's hat to counteract the influence of the centre of gravity when one falls out of a window or off a precipice, the result of which will be that the person who falls off one of these high places will drop down slowly, and not with the rapidity which at the present day is responsible for the dreadful outcome of accidents of that sort. Then, finally—"

"You pretend to be able to penetrate to the finality, do you?" asked the Clergyman.

"Why not? It is as easy to imagine the finality as it is to go half-way there," returned the Idiot. "Finally he will tackle some elementary principle of nature, and he'll blow the world to smithereens."

There was silence at the table. This at least seemed to be a tenable theory. That man should have the temerity to take liberties with elementary principles was quite within reason, man being an animal of rare conceit, and that the result would bring about destruction was not at all at variance with probability.

"I believe it's happened once or twice already," said the Idiot.

"Do you really?" asked Mr. Pedagog, with a show of interest. "Upon what do you base this belief?"

"Well, take Africa," said the Idiot. "Take North America. What do we find? We find in the sands of the Sahara a great statue, which we call the Sphinx, and about which we know nothing, except that it is there and that it keeps its mouth shut. We find marvellous creations in engineering that to-day surpass anything that we can do. The Sphinx, when discovered, was covered by sand. Now I believe that at one time there were people much further advanced in science than ourselves, who made these wonderful things, who knew how to do things that we don't even dream of doing, and I believe that they, like this creature I have predicted, got fooling with the centre of gravity, and that the world slipped its moorings for a period of time, during which time it tumbled topsy-turvey into space, and that banks and banks of sand and water and ice thrown out of position simply swept on and over the whole surface of the globe continuously until the earth got into the grip of the rest of the universe once more and started along in a new orbit. We know that where we are high and dry to-day the

ocean must once have rolled. We know that
where the world is now all sunshine and flow-
ers great glaciers stood. What caused all
this change? Nothing else, in my judgment, than the monkeying of man with the
forces of nature. The poles changed, and it
wouldn't surprise me a bit that, if the north
pole were ever found and could be thawed
out, we should find embedded in that great
sea of ice evidences of a former civilization,
just as in the Saharan waste evidences of the
same thing have been found. I know of a
place out West that is literally strewn with
oyster-shells, and yet no man living has the
slightest idea how they came there. It may
have been the Massachusetts Bay of a pre-
historic time, for all we know. It may have
been an antediluvian Coney Island, for all the
world knows. Who shall say that this little
upset of mine found here an oyster-bed,
shook all the oysters out of their bed into
space, and left their clothes high and dry in
a locality which, but for those garments,
would seem never to have known the oyster
in his prime? Off in Westchester County, on
the top of a high hill, lies a rock, and in the
uppermost portion of that rock is a so-called
pot-hole, made by nothing else than the drop-

ping of water of a brook and the swirling of
pebbles therein. It is now beyond the reach
of anything in the shape of water save that
which falls from the heavens. It is certain
that this pot-hole was never made by a boy
with a watering-pot, by a hired man with a
hose, by a workman with a drill, or by any
rain-storm that ever fell in Westchester County. There must at some time or another have
been a stream there; and as streams do not
flow uphill and bore pot-holes on mountain-
tops, there must have been a valley there.
Some great cataclysm took place. For that
cataclysm nature must be held responsible
mainly. But what prompted nature to raise
hob with Westchester County millions of
years ago, and to let it sleep like Rip Van
Winkle ever since? Nature isn't a freak.
She is depicted as a woman, but in spite of
that she is not whimsical. She does not act
upon impulses. There must have been some
cause for her behavior in turning valleys into
hills, in transforming huge cities into wastes
of sand, and oyster-beds into shell quarries;
and it is my belief that man was the contributing cause. He tapped the earth for natural
gas; he bored in and he bored out, and he
bored nature to death, and then nature rose

up and smote him and his cities and his oyster-beds, and she'll do it again unless we go slow."

"There is a great deal in what you say," said Mr. Whitechoker.

"Very true," said Mrs. Pedagog. "But I wish he'd stop saying it. The last three dozen cakes have got cold as ice while he was talking, and I can't afford such reckless waste."

"Nor we, Mrs. Pedagog," said the Idiot, with a pleasant smile; "for, as I was saying to the Bibliomaniac this morning, your buckwheat cakes are, to my mind, the very highest development of our modern civilization, and to have even one of them wasted seems to me to be a crime against Nature herself, for which a second, third, or fourth shaking up of this earth would be an inadequate punishment."

This remark so pleased Mrs. Pedagog that she ordered the cook to send up a fresh lot of cakes; and the guests, after eating them, adjourned to their various duties with light hearts, and digestions occupied with work of great importance.

XI

I WONDER what would have happened if Columbus had not discovered America?" said the Bibliomaniac, as the company prepared to partake of the morning meal.

"He would have gone home disappointed," said the Idiot, with a look of surprise on his face, which seemed to indicate that in his opinion the Bibliomaniac was very dull-witted not to have solved the problem for himself. "He would have gone home disappointed, and we would now be foreigners, like most other Americans. Mr. Pedagog would doubtless be instructing the young scions of the aristocracy of Tipperary, Mr. Whitechoker would be Archbishop of Canterbury, the Bibliomaniac would be raising bulbs in Holland, and—"

"And you would be wandering about with the other wild men of Borneo at the present time," put in the School-Master.

"THE BIBLIOMANIAC WOULD BE RAISING BULBS"

"No," said the Idiot. "Not quite. I should be dividing my time up between Holland, France, Switzerland, and Spain."

"You are an international sort of Idiot, eh?" queried the Lawyer, with a chuckle at his own wit.

"Say rather a cosmopolitan Idiot," said the Idiot. "Among my ancestors I number individuals of various nations, though I suppose that if we go back far enough we were all in the same boat as far as that is concerned. One of my great-great-grandfathers was a Scotchman, one of them was a Dutchman, another was a Spaniard, a fourth was a Frenchman. What the others were I don't know. It's a nuisance looking up one's ancestors, I think. They increase so as you go back into the past. Every man has had two grandfathers, four great-grandfathers, eight great-great-grandfathers, sixteen great-great-great-grandfathers, thirty-two fathers raised to the fourth power of great-grandness, and so on, increasing in number as you go further back, until it is hardly possible for any one to throw a brick into the pages of history without hitting somebody who is more or less responsible for his existence. I dare say there is a streak of Julius Cæsar in me, and I

haven't a doubt that if our friend **Mr. Peda-**
gog here were to take the trouble to investi-
gate, he would find that **Cæsar** and **Cassius**
and **Brutus** could be numbered among his
early progenitors—and now that I think of it,
I must say that in my estimation he is an unusually amiable man, considering how diverse
the nature of these men were. Think of it
for a minute. Here a man unites in himself
Cæsar and Cassius and Brutus, two of whom
killed the third, and then, having quarrelled
together, went out upon a battle - field and
slaughtered themselves, after making extem-
poraneous remarks, for which this miserable
world gives Shakespeare all the credit. It's
worse than the case of a friend of mine, one
of whose grandfathers was French and the
other German."

"How did it affect him?" asked **Mr. White-**
choker.

"It made him distrust himself," said the
Idiot, with a smile, "and for that reason he
never could get on in the world. When his
Teutonic nature suggested that he do something, his Gallic blood would rise up and spoil
everything, and *vice versa.* He was eternally
quarrelling with himself. He was a victim to
internal disorder of the worst sort."

"And what, pray, finally became of him?" asked the Clergyman.

"He shot himself in a duel," returned the Idiot, with a wink at the genial old gentleman who occasionally imbibed. "It was very sad."

"I've known sadder things," said Mr. Pedagog, wearily. "Your elaborate jokes, for instance. They are enough to make strong men weep."

"You flatter me, Mr. Pedagog," said the Idiot. "I have never in all my experience as a cracker of jests made a man laugh until he cried, but I hope to some day. But, really, do you know I think Columbus is an immensely overrated man. If you come down to it, what did he do? He went out to sea in a ship and sailed for three months, and when he least expected it ran slam-bang up against the Western Hemisphere. It was like shooting at a barn door with a Gatling gun. He was bound to hit it sooner or later."

"You don't give him any credit for tenacity of purpose or good judgment, then?" asked Mr. Brief.

"Of course I do. Plenty of it. He stuck to his ship like a hero who didn't know how to swim. His judgment was great. He had too much sense to go back to Spain without any news of something, because he fully understood that unless he had something to show for the trip, there would have been a great laugh on Queen Isabella for selling her jewels to provide for a ninety-day yacht cruise for him and a lot of common sailors, which would never have done. So he kept on and on, and finally some unknown lookout up in the bow discovered America. Then Columbus went home and told everybody that if it hadn't been for his own eagle eye emigration wouldn't have been invented, and world's fairs would have been local institutions. Then they got up a parade in which the King and Queen graciously took part, and Columbus became a great man. Meanwhile the unknown lookout who did discover the land was knocking about the town and thinking he was a very lucky fellow to get an extra glass of grog. It wasn't anything more than the absolute justice of fate that caused the new land to be named America and not Columbia. It really ought to have been named after that fellow up in the bow."

"But, my dear Idiot," put in the Bibliomaniac, "the scheme itself was Columbus's own. He evolved the theory that the earth is round like a ball."

"To quote Mr. Pedagog—" began the Idiot.

"You can't quote me in your own favor," snapped the School-Master.

"Wait until I have finished," said the Idiot. "I was only going to quote you by saying 'Tutt!' that's all; and so I repeat, in the words of Mr. Pedagog, tutt, tutt! Evolved the theory? Why, man, how could he help evolving the theory? There was the sun rising in the east every morning and setting in the west every night. What else was there to believe? That somebody put the sun out every night, and sneaked back east with it under cover of darkness?"

"But you forget that the wise men of the day laughed at his idea," said Mr. Pedagog, surveying the Idiot after the fashion of a man who has dealt an adversary a stinging blow.

"That only proves what I have always said," replied the Idiot. "Wise men can't find fun in anything but stern facts. Wise men always do laugh at truth. Whenever I advance some new proposition, you sit up there next to Mrs. Pedagog and indulge in tutt-tutterances of the most intolerant sort. If you had been one of the wise men of Columbus's time there isn't any doubt in my mind that when Columbus said the earth was round, you'd have remarked tutt, tutt, in Spanish." There was silence for a minute, and then the Idiot began again. "There's another point about this whole business that makes me tired," he said. "It only goes to prove the conceit of these Europeans. Here was a great continent inhabited by countless people. A European comes over here and is said to be the discoverer of America and is glorified. Statues of him are scattered broadcast all over the world. Pictures of him are printed in the newspapers and magazines. A dozen different varieties of portraits of him are printed on postage-stamps as big as circus posters—and all for what? Because he discovered a land that millions of Indians had known about for centuries. On the other hand, when Columbus goes back to Spain several of the native Americans trust their precious lives to his old tubs. One of these savages must have been the first American to discover Europe. Where are the statues of the Indian who discovered Europe? Where are the postage-stamps showing how he looked

on the day when Europe first struck his vis-
ion ? Where is anybody spending a billion
of dollars getting up a world's fair in com-
memoration of Lo's discovery of Europe?"

"He didn't know it was Europe," said the
Bibliomaniac.

"Columbus didn't know this was America," retorted the Idiot. "In fact, Columbus
didn't know anything. He didn't know any
better than to write a letter to Queen Isabella and mail it in a keg that never turned up.
He didn't even know how to steer his old
boat into a real solid continent, instead of
getting ten days on the island. He was an
awfully wise man. He saw an island swarm-
ing with Indians, and said, 'Why, this must
be India!' And worst of all, if his pictures
mean anything, he didn't even know enough
to choose his face and stick to it. Don't talk
Columbus to me unless you want to prove
that luck is the greatest factor of success."

"Ill-luck is sometimes a factor of success,"
said Mr. Pedagog. "You are a success as
an Idiot, which appears to me to be extremely unfortunate."

"I don't know about that," said the Idiot.
"I adapt myself to my company, and of
course—"

"Then you are a school-master among school-masters, a lawyer among lawyers, and so forth?" queried the Bibliomaniac.

"What are you when your company is made up of widely diverse characters?" asked Mr. Brief before the Idiot had a chance to reply to the Bibliomaniac's question.

"I try to be a widely diverse character myself."

"And, trying to sit on many stools, fall and become just an Idiot," said Mr. Pedagog.

"That's according to the way you look at it. I put my company to the test in the crucible of my mind. I analyze the characters of all about me, and whatever quality predominates in the precipitate, that I become. Thus in the presence of my employer and his office-boy I become a mixture of both—something of the employer, something of an office-boy. I run errands for my employer, and boss the office-boy. With you gentlemen I go through the same process. The Bibliomaniac, the School-Master, Mr. Brief, and the rest of you have been cast into the crucible, and I have tried to approximate the result."

"And are an Idiot," said the School-Master.

"It is your own name for me, gentlemen,"

"DIDN'T KNOW ENOUGH TO CHOOSE HIS OWN FACE"

returned the Idiot. " I presume you have recognized your composite self, and have chosen the title accordingly."

" You were a little hard on me this morning, weren't you ?" asked the genial old gentleman who occasionally imbibed, that evening, when he and the Idiot were discussing the morning's chat. " I didn't like to say anything about it, but I don't think you ought to have thrown me into the crucible with the rest."

" I wish you had spoken," said the Idiot, warmly. " It would have given me a chance to say that the grain of sense that once or twice a year leavens the lump of my idiocy is directly due to the ingredient furnished by yourself. Here's to you, old man. If you and I lived alone together, what a wise man I should be !"

And then the genial old gentleman went to the cupboard and got out a bottle of port-wine that he had been preserving in cobwebs for ten years. This he opened, and as he did so he said, " I've been keeping this for years, my boy. It was dedicated in my youth to the thirst of the first man who truly appreciated me. Take it all."

"I'll divide with you," returned the Idiot, with a smile. "For really, old fellow, I think you—ah—I think you appreciate yourself as much as I do."

XII

" I wonder what it costs to run a flat ?"
said the Idiot, stirring his coffee with the
salt-spoon — a proceeding which seemed to
indicate that he was thinking of something
else.

" Don't you keep an expense account ?"
asked the Bibliomaniac, slyly.

" Hee-hee !" laughed Mrs. Pedagog.

" First - rate joke," said the Idiot, with a
smile. " But really, now, I should like to
know for how little an apartment could be
run. I am interested."

Mrs. Pedagog stopped laughing at once.
The Idiot's words were ominous. She did
not always like his views, but she did like
his money, and she was not at all anxious to
lose him as a boarder.

" It's very expensive," she said, firmly. " I
shouldn't ever advise any one to undertake
living in a flat. Rents are high. Butcher

bills are enormous, because the butchers have to pay commissions, not only to the cook, so that she'll use twice as much lard as she can, and give away three or four times as much to the poor as she ought, but janitors have to be seen to, and elevator-boys, and all that. Groceries come high for the same reason. Oh, no! Flat life isn't the life for anybody, I say. Give me a good, first-class boarding-house. Am I not right, John ?"

"Yes, indeed," said Mr. Pedagog. "Every time. I lived in a flat once, and it was an awful nuisance. Above me lived a dancing-master who gave lessons at every hour of the day in the room directly over my study, so that I was always being disturbed at my work, while below me was a music-teacher who was practising all night, so that I could hardly sleep. Worst of all, on the same floor with me was a miserable person of convivial tendencies, who always mistook my door for his when he came home after midnight, and who gave some quite estimable people two floors below to believe that it was I, and not he, who sang comic songs between three and four o'clock in the morning. There has not been too much love lost between the Idiot and myself, but I cannot be so vin-

" JANITORS HAVE TO BE SEEN TO '

dictive as to recommend him to live in a flat."

"I can bear testimony to the same effect," put in Mr. Brief, who was two weeks in arrears, and anxious to conciliate his landlady.

"Testimony to the effect that Mr. Pedagog sang comic songs in the early morning?" said the Idiot. "Nonsense! I don't believe it. I have lived in this house for two years with Mr. Pedagog, and I've never heard him raise his voice in song yet."

"I didn't mean anything of the sort," retorted Mr. Brief. "You know I didn't."

"Don't apologize to me," said the Idiot. "Apologize to Mr. Pedagog. He is the man you have wronged."

"What did he say?" put in Mr. Pedagog, with a stern look at Mr. Brief. "I didn't hear what he said."

"I didn't say anything," said the lawyer, "except that I could bear testimony to the effect that your experience with flat life was similar to mine. This young person, with his customary nerve, tries to make it appear that I said you sang comic songs in the early morning."

"I try to do nothing of the sort," said the Idiot. "I simply expressed my belief that in spite of what you said Mr. Pedagog was innocent, and I do so because my experience with him has taught me that he is not the kind of man who would do that sort of thing. He has neither time, voice, nor inclination. He has an ear—two of them, in fact—and an impressionable mind; but—"

"Oh, tutt!" interrupted the School-Master. "When I need a defender, you may spare yourself the trouble of flying to my rescue."

"I know I *may*," said the Idiot, "but with me it's a question of can and can't. I'm willing to attack you personally, but while I live no other shall do so. Wherefore I tell Mr. Brief plainly, and to his face, that if he says you ever sang a comic song he says what is not so. You might hum one, but sing it—never!"

"We were talking of flats, I believe," said Mr. Whitechoker.

"Yes," said the Idiot, "and these persons have changed it from flat talk to sharp talk."

"Well, anyhow," put in Mr. Brief, "I lived in a flat once, and it was anything but pleasant. I lost a case once for the simple and only reason that I lived in a flat. It was a case that required a great deal of strategy on my part, and I invited my client to my home to unfold my plan of action. I got interested in the scheme as I unfolded it, and spoke in my usual impassioned manner, as though addressing a jury, and, would you believe it, the opposing counsel happened to be visiting a friend on the next floor, and my eloquence floated up through the air-shaft, and gave our whole plan of action away. We were routed on the point we had supposed would pierce the enemy's armor and lay him at our feet, for the wholly simple reason that that abominable air-shaft had made my strategic move a matter of public knowledge."

"That's a good idea for a play," said the Idiot. "A roaring farce could be built up on that basis. Villain and accomplice on one floor, innocent victim on floor above. Plot floats up air-shaft. Innocent victim overhears; villain and accomplice say 'ha ha' for three acts and take a back seat in the fourth, with a grand transformation showing the conspirators in the county jail as a finale. Write it up with lots of live-stock wandering in and out, bring in janitors and elevator-boys and butchers, show up some of the humors of flat life, if there be any such, call it *A Hole in the Flat*, and put it on the stage.

Nine hundred nights is the very shortest run it could have, which at fifty dollars a night for the author is $45,000 in good hard dollars. Mr. Poet, the idea is yours for a fiver. Say the word."

"Thanks," said the Poet, with a smile ; "I'm not a dramatist."

"Then I'll have to do it myself," said the Idiot. "And if I do, good-bye Shakespeare."

"That's so," said Mr. Pedagog. Nothing could more effectually ruin the dramatic art than to have you write a play. People, seeing your work, would say, here, this will never do. The stage must be discouraged at all costs. A hypocrite throws the ministry into disgrace, an ignoramus brings shame upon education, and an unpopular lawyer gives the bar a bad name. I think you are just the man to ruin Shakespeare."

"Then I'll give up my ambition to become a playwright and stick to idiocy," said the Idiot. "But to come back to flats. Your feeling in regard to them is entirely different from that of a friend of mine, who has lived in one for ten years. He thinks flat life is ideal. His children can't fall down-stairs, because there aren't any stairs to fall down. His roof never leaks, because he hasn't any

"MY ELOQUENCE FLOATED UP THE AIR-SHAFT"

roof to leak ; and when he and his family want to go off anywhere, all he has to do is to lock his front door and go. Burglars never climb into his front window, because they are all eight flights up. Damp cellars don't trouble him, because they are too far down to do him any injury, even if they overflow. The cares of house-keeping are reduced to a minimum. His cook doesn't spend all her time in the front area flirting with the postman, because there isn't any front area to his flat ; and in a social way his wife is most delightfully situated, because most of her friends live in the same building, and instead of having to hire a carriage to go calling in, all she has to do is to take the elevator and go from one floor to another. If he pines for a change of scene, he is high enough up in the air to get it by looking out of his windows, over the tops of other buildings, into the green fields to the north, or looking westward into the State of New Jersey. Instead of taking a drive through the Park, or a walk, all he and his wife need to do is to take a telescope and follow some little sylvan path with their eyes. Then, as for expense, he finds that he saves money by means of a co-operative scheme. For instance, if he wants shad for dinner, and he and his wife cannot eat a whole one, he goes shares on the shad and its cost with his neighbors above and below."

" Yes, and his neighbors above and below borrow tea and eggs and butter and ice and other things whenever they run short, so that in that way he loses all he saves," said Mr. Pedagog, resolved not to give in.

" He does if he isn't smart," said the Idiot. "I thought of that myself, and asked him about it, and he told me that he kept account of all that, and always made it a point after some neighbor had borrowed two pounds of butter from him to send in before the week was over and borrow three pounds of butter from the neighbor. So far his books show that he is sixteen pounds of butter, seven pounds of tea, one bottle of vanilla extract, and a ton of ice ahead of the whole house. He is six eggs and a box of matches behind in his egg and match account, but under the circumstances I think he can afford it."

" But," said Mrs. Pedagog, anxious to know the worst, " why—er—why are you so interested ?"

" Well," said the Idiot, slowly, " I—er—I am contemplating a change, Mrs. Pedagog—

a change that would fill me—I say it sincere-
ly, too—with regret if—" The Idiot paused
a minute, and his eye swept fondly about the
table. His voice was getting a little husky
too, Mr. Whitechoker noticed. "It would
fill me with regret, I say, if it were not that
in taking up house-keeping I am — I am to
have the assistance of a better-half."

"What?" cried the Bibliomaniac. "You?
You are going to be—to be married?"

"Why not?" said the Idiot. "Imitation
is the sincerest flattery. Mr. Pedagog mar-
ries, and I am going to flatter him as sincere-
ly as I can by following in his footsteps."

"May I—may we ask to whom?" asked
Mrs. Pedagog, softly.

"Certainly," said the Idiot. "To Mr. Barlow's daughter. Mr. Barlow is — or was—
my employer."

"Was? Is he not now? Are you going
out of business?" asked Mr. Pedagog.

"No ; but, you see, when I went to see
Mr. Barlow in the matter, he told me that he
liked me very much, and he had no doubt I
would make a good husband for his daughter, but, after all, he added that I was nothing but a confidential clerk on a small salary,
and he thought his daughter could do better."

"She couldn't find a better fellow, Mr. Idiot," said Mrs. Pedagog, and Mr. Pedagog rose to the occasion by nodding his entire acquiescence in the statement.

"Thank you very much," said the Idiot." "That was precisely what I told Mr. Barlow, and I suggested a scheme to him by which his sole objection could be got around."

"You would start in business for yourself?" said Mr. Whitechoker.

"In a sense, yes," said the Idiot. "Only the way I put it was that a good confidential clerk would make a good partner for him, and he, after thinking it over, thought I was right."

"It certainly was a characteristically novel way out of the dilemma," said Mr. Brief, with a smile.

"I thought so myself, and so did he, so it was all arranged. On the 1st of next month I enter the firm, and on the 15th I am—ah— to be married."

The company warmly congratulated the Idiot upon his good - fortune, and he shortly left the room, more overcome by their felicitations than he had been by their arguments in the past.

The few days left passed quickly by, and

there came a breakfast at Mrs. Pedagog's house that was a mixture of joy and sadness —joy for his happiness, sadness that that table should know the Idiot no more.

Among the wedding-gifts was a handsomely bound series of volumes, including a cyclopædia, a dictionary, and a little tome of poems, the first output of the Poet. These came together, with a card inscribed, "From your Friends of the Breakfast Table," of whom the Idiot said, when Mrs. Idiot asked for information :

"They, my dear, next to yourself and my parents, are the dearest friends I ever had. We must have them up to breakfast some morning."

"Breakfast ?" queried Mrs. Idiot.

"Yes, my dear," he replied, simply. "I should be afraid to meet them at any other meal. I am always at my best at breakfast, and they—well, they never are."

THE END

Reprint Publishing

FOR PEOPLE WHO GO FOR ORIGINALS.

This book is a facsimile reprint of the original edition. The term refers to the facsimile with an original in size and design exactly matching simulation as photographic or scanned reproduction.

Facsimile editions offer us the chance to join in the library of historical, cultural and scientific history of mankind, and to rediscover.

The books of the facsimile edition may have marks, notations and other marginalia and pages with errors contained in the original volume. These traces of the past refers to the historical journey that has covered the book.

ISBN 978-3-95940-061-9

Made in Germany

www.reprintpublishing.com

www.ingramcontent.com/pod-product-compliance
Lightning Source LLC
Chambersburg PA
CBHW051128260626
47170CB00005B/1709